# Whirlwind

## BOOK FIVE OF
## DREAMHOUSE KINGS

# ROBERT LIPARULO

## THOMAS NELSON
### Since 1798

NASHVILLE  DALLAS  MEXICO CITY  RIO DE JANEIRO

Published in Nashville, Tennessee by Thomas Nelson. Thomas Nelson is a registered trademark of Thomas Nelson, Inc.

Page design by Mandi Cofer
Map design by Doug Cordes

Thomas Nelson, Inc., books may be purchased in bulk for educational, business, fund-raising, or sales promotional use. For information, please e-mail SpecialMarkets@ThomasNelson.com.

ISBN 978-1-59554-892-4 (trade paper)

### Library of Congress Cataloging-in-Publication Data

Liparulo, Robert.
  Whirlwind / Robert Liparulo.
     p. cm. — (Dreamhouse Kings ; bk. 5)
  Summary: To save the world from destruction, rescue their kidnapped mother, and battle the evil Taksidian, the King siblings try to control the mysterious portals in their house that send them to different time periods.
  ISBN 978-1-59554-815-3 (hard cover)
  [1. Time travel—Fiction. 2. Dwellings—Fiction. 3. Brothers and sisters—Fiction. 4. Supernatural—Fiction.] I. Title.
  PZ7.L6636Wh 2009
  [Fic]—dc22

                              2009041500

*Printed in the United States of America*
10 11 12 13 RRD 5 4 3 2 1

THIS ONE IS FOR MY PARENTS,
MAE GANNON AND
TONY LIPARULO

*Thank you for instilling in me the belief that my imagination
could take me anywhere: Turns out, it has taken me everywhere.*

# STOP!

READ *HOUSE OF DARK SHADOWS,*
*WATCHER IN THE WOODS,*
*GATEKEEPERS,* AND *TIMESCAPE*
BEFORE CONTINUING!

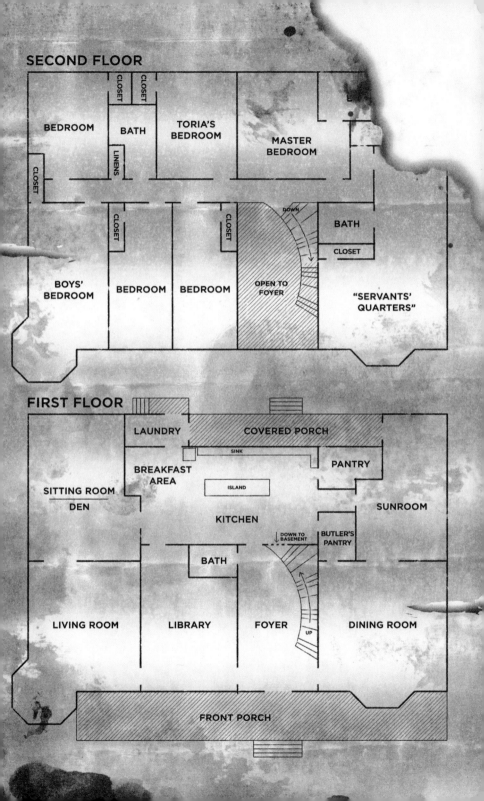

*"All that is necessary for evil to succeed
is that good men do nothing."*

—EDMUND BURKE

*"The Universe is stranger than we can imagine."*

—BILL BRYSON

# CHAPTER

## one

David King's scream echoed against the chamber walls.

Loud in his ears, but not loud enough. He could tell by the way it bounced back at him that his voice did not penetrate the thick stones. He leaned back against a cold wall.

Lifting his head, he screamed again anyway: "Heeeeeeeelp! Can anyone hear me? Anyone . . . ?"

1

The last word started strong, but faded, like the shriek of a man falling into a bottomless pit.

Darkness—blacker than ink—engulfed him, but it didn't matter: he kept his eyes squeezed shut, as though doing so would make the last thing he'd seen not be real, would make it go away. He was stuck in a room only slightly larger than an upended coffin, portaled there from a pantry off Taksidian's kitchen. He had found a box of matches on a protruding stone and lit one. He had seen that the floor was covered in bones. Most of them—rib cages, spines, skulls—had been pulverized into gravel-like pellets and dust. Only near the walls were the remains intact enough to recognize, as though feet had stomped around on a roomful of skeletons . . . before whoever had been trapped before him died and decayed, adding their own bones to the floor.

Starvation. Lack of air. Heart attack from fright. He could think of a dozen ways to die in a place like this.

The walls all around were made of gray stone, cut into eight-inch cubes and fitted together so perfectly he couldn't wedge a fingernail between them. Moisture had formed or was running down over them, making David think of underground crypts.

*Dracula's castle*, he thought, and before he could stop it, the image of a white-faced vampire drifted out of the darkness of his imagination. His breath caught in his throat. Had something shifted in the small space? Something that wasn't him? There *was* enough room for another person, another *thing*.

*Stop!* he told himself. *Where would someone else come from? Get real.*

But his mind answered: *The floor, rising up from the bones of its victims.*

Or from the same place he had come, Taksidian's house!

Taksidian was the man who wanted his family's home. He wanted them out or wanted them dead. David was pretty sure Taksidian didn't care which, as long as he had the place for himself. Soon after moving into it—*just over a week ago!* David realized, though it seemed like years—they had found a secret third floor and a hallway lined with doors. Behind each door was a small room, an antechamber, with items that, when picked up or put on, opened another door. This other door, one for each room, was really a portal to another time and place.

His brother, Xander, had been the first to "go over," as they called stepping through the portals. He'd wound up in the Roman Colosseum, fighting a gladiator. Then they discovered that not only could they go from the house to other "worlds," but people from those other places could come into their house. And one did: a hulking brute who kidnapped Mom and took her *somewhere* . . . somewhere in time. They'd been trying to find her ever since.

"Hello?" David said into the darkness, listening to his

voice bounce off the walls. If someone had answered, he would have dropped dead on the spot. But no one did. No vampire, no Taksidian.

Taksidian. He had first offered to buy the house, then got the cops to arrest Dad and persuaded the town officials that the house was unsafe. David couldn't argue with that one. When those tricks hadn't worked, the man had somehow sent people from the past to get them—that big brute, the one Xander had dubbed Phemus, and two of his buddies.

David stared into the darkness and groaned. It had been a *long* week, with enough adventure and brushes with death to fill a lifetime. The latest one had begun just a few hours ago.

He, Xander, and Dad had followed Taksidian to his house way back in the woods. When Taksidian took off, Dad went after him and the boys broke into the house. They discovered a room full of maps, photos, and articles—all of them about war throughout history. Except one wall. It was covered with photos of the King family going about their daily lives, and maps of their house, and notes written in a foreign language.

That's when Taksidian had returned, and the brothers had scrambled to hide: Xander had gone into a bedroom, David into a pantry—which had immediately shot him into this dark chamber . . .

*How can that be? It can't! It can't!*

David prayed his brother was all right, that he'd gotten away. Somehow.

A thought struck him like the blade of a shovel: *What if Taksidian's entire house is filled with portals, like our house's third floor? What if it's like a big hunk of Swiss cheese, just waiting for people to fall into a hole and disappear?*

But to where? Where was he?

David opened his eyes. He had to blink to make sure he had really opened them and not just thought about doing it; the blackness was that complete. Tears spilled down his cheeks, and he wiped them away.

Remembering that he'd imagined someone in the chamber with him, he stuck out his arms, moved them around. Taksidian *could* have come through after him, even though David had thought he'd gotten into the pantry without being seen. When he felt nothing but air, he let out a breath he didn't know he had been holding.

He turned to the wall and pounded on it. Each blow landed with a *thud*, as solid and unrewarding as slamming his fist against a concrete sidewalk.

"Xander!" he yelled, thinking maybe, just maybe, he was still in Taksidian's house somewhere, and his brother would hear him.

He stepped back. The bones under his feet crunched, and he tried not to think about them. A plaster cast—crumbling, thanks to David's plunge into the Atlantic Ocean after he'd been dragged through a portal to the sinking *Titanic*—ran from his left hand to his elbow. Dad had wrapped an Ace bandage around it to keep it together. The skin underneath itched like a thousand ants were swarming over it. Deep within, his bone ached.

He realized he was holding something in that hand: the box of matches. He pushed it open and pulled out a stick. He touched the match head to the side of the box, and thought, *Do I really want to see? Walls, that's all that's here . . . and skulls.*

Like the one that had been glaring up at him with big black sockets last time he'd lit a match. A memory popped into his head. Something from Ancient Civ: the Aztecs or Incas or Mayans—he could never keep them straight—had used a human head as a ball in their version of soccer. He and Robbie, his best friend back in Pasadena, had joked that they'd like to do that with their soccer coach's head when he was in their faces more than usual. The thought turned David's stomach, not only because of the grossness of it, but because of the memory of Robbie and soccer and better times . . . *normal* times.

He pushed the matches into his pants pocket and pressed his palm to the wall. He lowered his head as his breathing turned into short, ragged gasps.

*Don't cry*, he told himself. *There's already been too much of that.*

But twelve years of living had not prepared him for this. Not any of it: Mom being kidnapped, a really bad guy trying to kill them, getting stuck in a chamber of bones. Forget that he was twelve: *nobody* could handle this.

6

The thought led to another: What were the options, if not to handle it? Give up. Just sit down and die.

No, that wasn't him. He wasn't ready to die yet.

He gritted his teeth and slapped the stones. Then he slapped them harder. His hand squeezed into a fist, and he punched the wall. He kicked it.

"Help," he said. He raised his face and yelled the word. Yelled it again . . . and again . . . and again . . .

CHAPTER

THURSDAY, AT THE SAME TIME

For a few seconds, it didn't matter to Xander that Taksidian, knife at the ready, had just burst into the room. All Xander could think about was the hideous sculpture he had backed into: a pillar of severed human body parts, all stacked and stuck together like a demonic version of Jenga.

But whatever had bonded them bound them no longer; as he toppled, loose arms, legs, fingers, ears fell with him. Something struck his cheek, sticky-wet, reeking. He landed on the parts of the sculpture that had fallen with him to the floor. Some pieces were hard, like logs; others squished under him, like oversized sausages.

His head cracked against the hardwood floor, and he lay there, stunned. The ceiling was blood red, with small spot-lights glaring down on the items mounted to black-painted walls: weapons, face masks, an ancient soldier's uniform. A tight constellation of bulbs cast a white glow into the center of the room, where the sculpture had stood.

He thought about what else was in the room: Jesse's finger, sitting on a stainless steel cart, waiting to be added to the sculpture. Jesse was Xander's great-great-uncle. He had built their house with his father and brother and had spent fifty years hopping in and out of history, doing . . . *whatever*—Jesse hadn't explained it, said there was plenty of time for that. Turned out there wasn't: the day after Jesse had arrived, Taksidian stabbed him and took his finger. Now Xander knew why.

As his senses came back, he thought of David, hoped he was out of the house and running as fast as his little soccer legs could carry him. Xander mentally kicked himself: he had been stupid to think they could break into Taksidian's house and get away with it. Dae had been scared, but he'd always been able to push his fear aside to do courageous things—like tagging along with his stupid older brother. David deserved to live, even if God had other plans for Xander.

When he lifted his head, he saw that an arm—not his—rested on his chest. Its open stub, showing a bull's-eye of bone surrounded by muscle and flesh, gaped not three inches from his chin. He made a gagging sound and swatted it away.

He rose and propped himself up with his arms, palms flat on the floor behind him. One of his sneakered feet rested on the black cube that had been the sculpture's pedestal. He squinted at his other foot, which was bare, and wondered how the fall could have knocked off his sneaker and sock. Then he realized that the foot was ghostly white, with blackened toe-nails; it was attached to a leg that ended before it reached a knee. He gasped and kicked, flipping the leg away.

Taksidian shifted—moving his knife from one hand to the other—drawing Xander's eyes back to him. He was simply standing there in the doorway. His black slicker was unbuttoned, revealing gray slacks and a pinstriped shirt. Like any Joe Schmo businessman, Xander thought. But he knew better.

"Wha-what is this?" Xander said, throwing a quick glance at the carnage around him. Pools of syrupy clear fluid were beginning to spread out from the pieces, glistening against the crimson-colored floor. The question was a diversion, some-thing to keep Taksidian from leaping at him with the knife. Xander already knew the answer, had seen enough movies to know: the body parts were trophies, which sick-minded serial killers took from their victims—to remember their crimes.

"Where I come from," Taksidian said, his voice deep and

smooth, "we honor our conquered enemies by turning a bit of them into . . . *art.*" His tight lips bent up at the corners. He surveyed the body parts, scattered around the room. "I'm afraid what you've done is like—" He looked up at the ceiling, thinking. "Like spray-painting graffiti all over the *Mona Lisa.*" He shook his head, said, "Terrible," and stepped closer.

Xander scrambled to stand. His foot slipped through a pool of liquid, and he sat down again, hard. He got his feet under him and rose. "Is that Jesse's?" he yelled, shakily pointing at a white finger resting on the metal cart. "You took his finger! That's it, isn't it?" More stalling. He scanned the room, looking for a way out, but the window, which would have been right behind him, had been bricked up. Taksidian blocked the only exit.

Taksidian glanced at the finger. "I don't think he'll be needing it anymore, do you?"

"He—" Xander started, wanting to throw it in Taksidian's face that Jesse was still alive—lying in a hospital bed, barely breathing, but alive. But he clamped his mouth tight, realizing it would do Jesse no good for Taksidian to know he hadn't finished the job. Quietly, Xander said, "He was a good man."

Taksidian gave him a one-shouldered shrug, as if to say, *So?* What he did say was colder still: "I respect your appreciation of him. I'll be sure to put something of *you* next to your uncle's finger, when I put my art back together." He eyed

Xander's arms and legs, taking his time appraising each one, as if he were shopping for a tie.

Xander spun to his right and leaped toward the wall of weapons. The nearest piece was a battered metal shield—*A shield!* his mind groaned. *Why not a knife, a sword like the one too close to Taksidian to reach?* He yanked the shield off the wall and almost dropped it. It was a lot heavier than it looked. He swung it around, expecting to make contact with Taksidian.

But the man hadn't moved from his spot on the other side of the room. He watched Xander with bored eyes, the knife gripped in a hand that hung down by his leg.

"Back off!" Xander said, hefting the shield up with both hands, pumping it toward Taksidian. He glanced into the shallow concavity of the shield's back side and saw a leather strap and metal handhold. Straining his muscles to hold the shield with one hand, he slipped his left arm through the strap and grabbed the handle. The shield seemed to get lighter, as though it had been carefully balanced to minimize arm stress when held properly. His right hand was now free. He flicked his eyes toward the next item on the wall: a long stick with a starburst of six-inch spikes jutting from one end.

When his gaze bounced back to Taksidian, he realized the man was now three feet closer. Xander had not taken his eyes off him for more than a half second. The guy moved almost magically, without the slightest warning or wobble. Standing ramrod straight one instant, three feet closer the next.

"Whoa!" Xander said. He swung the shield out and back, like opening and closing a door, trying to show Taksidian what he was in for if he moved closer. His guts shifted inside as he grasped the reason for the man's calmness: Taksidian was a killer, and he was *good* at it. He knew the moves, could perform them as easily as breathing.

A feeling of hopelessness washed over Xander. Who was he next to this guy? An ant to be squashed, nothing more. He wondered how it would happen. Maybe Taksidian would be standing in front of him before he knew it, the knife slipping effortlessly around the shield. Or the killer would torment him, moving in slowly, telling Xander the artistic merits of adding a fifteen-year-old ear, instead of a toe or arm, to the sculpture.

Xander felt his jaw muscles tighten. Out of the corner of his eye, he gauged the distance to the spike-studded stick, the number of steps he would need to reach it, the number of seconds. He could do it: leap, grab, swing.

*Keep the shield up*, he told himself. That's what Russell Crowe, the *Gladiator* himself, would do. Xander searched his memory for something else useful. But this wasn't the movies, and nothing came to mind. Nothing except a quote that seemed about right. He couldn't remember who said it, Bruce Willis or Clint Eastwood or some other supertough guy.

Looking at Taksidian over the top of the shield, he narrowed his eyes. He nodded and said, "Bring it on, punk."

# CHAPTER

# three

## THURSDAY, AT THE SAME TIME

Ed King cranked the steering wheel of the VW Bug and pushed his foot harder on the gas pedal, which was already depressed all the way to the floor. The car nearly spun out on the dirt road leading up to Taksidian's place. It slid into the bushes; the sound of branches scraping the metal and glass matched the shrieking Mr. King had been hearing in his head from his jangled nerves. He swung the wheel around and got the car back on the road.

Taksidian had led him up into the hills on the other side of the highway, then doubled back, burning rubber to his house. He had somehow known David and Xander had stayed behind to snoop around.

"How?" Mr. King yelled out loud, smacking his palm against the wheel. "How did you know they were there?" He maneuvered through a hairpin turn in the road. The Bug's rear end slid sideways. It smacked against a boulder, spun its wheels, and took off again.

Not easy riding on two tireless wheel rims. By the time Mr. King had returned to the car to pursue Taksidian's Mercedes, the man had slashed the Bug's driver's-side tires. Mr. King had driven anyway, panicked to reach a place in the universe where his mobile phone worked: he *had* to warn his children about Taksidian! The flat tires had peeled away long ago, making the car lean to the left side as though Mr. King weighed eight hundred pounds, and turning steering into a game of chance. Sometimes the wheels obeyed his directions, but mostly they slid willy-nilly all over the road.

Still, he had done it. Down to the highway, a mile on black-top—the wheels wailing metallically like tortured robots—to Taksidian's long, winding drive, and—

*Almost there!* he thought. *Come on! Come on!*

The Bug fishtailed around the bend in the road where they had first hidden it in the bushes to approach the house on foot. There it was, the house, at the end of a long stretch of road. It was a simple place: single story, brick front, a patch of untended yard. The garage was on the very right side, a bay window—probably a living room—on the far left. Between them were a front door and a place where a window had been bricked up.

The wheel rims spun in the dirt, forcing the car to swerve left. The front end bounded off the road, heading for the dense woods that lined both sides of the drive. Mr. King yanked the wheel right, correcting the car. It picked up speed as it approached the house. The Mercedes was parked on the pad in front of the closed garage door.

He snatched his phone out of his shirt pocket and looked at the screen. He had service. He thumbed the speed-dial button for Xander.

# CHAPTER

# four

Taksidian smiled.

The response plucked at Xander's already frayed confidence. He swallowed and tried to hold his tough-guy expression.

*Do it,* he told himself. *Go for the spiky stick: leap, grab, swing.*

"How do you want it?" Taksidian asked. "Fast or slow?" He lowered and raised his eyelids, seemingly uninterested. "Either way's fine with me."

Trying not to warn Taksidian of his intentions, Xander slowly turned his hips toward the weapon. He leaned back slightly on his heels and angled his feet that way as well. He tilted his head, hoping to hide the way his body went down as he bent his knees.

Taksidian sighed. He looked at the weapon, then back at Xander.

Xander's heart sank. *Okay, he knows. Now what?* He thought about it and made a decision: *do it anyway.* But his body didn't spring into action, and his mind seemed okay with that. *Come on,* he thought. *On three. One . . .*

Music erupted, startling him. It was his cell phone, playing the soundtrack of *Fistful of Dollars.* His hand shot to his rear pocket, knowing Taksidian would take this opportunity to attack, would have to attack to stop him from answering the phone.

The man raised the knife and scratched his cheek with its tip. "Answer it," he said. "Tell your old man you need him. Yes, this might finish up faster than I thought."

Xander tugged the phone out, flipped it open. "Dad! He's here, Taksidian! He has a knife!"

"Where are you?" His father sounded out of breath.

"In the house! Dad—!"

"Where in the house, exactly?"

"What? Uh, a room . . . at the front. It has a bricked-up window. I can't get out!"

Taksidian pushed a strand of hair off his forehead with the knife tip.

"Xander," Dad said, "get away from the wall, where the window was."

"I—" Xander glanced over his shoulder at the wall on which the soldier's uniform was mounted. Getting away from it meant moving closer to Taksidian. "I can't. He—"

"Then duck!"

Xander got it. He dropped the phone.

Taksidian's eyes watched it fall. For the first time, he showed an emotion other than boredom. His brows scrunched together in puzzlement.

Both of them heard it, the high-pitched whine of an engine pushed way past its breaking point. In the space of an eye-blink, its volume doubled.

Xander dropped into a low crouch, spinning himself away from the wall. Pushing himself against a side wall, he pulled the shield up to his body. Just before he tucked his head behind it, he saw Taksidian's eyes flash wide.

The front wall exploded.

The sound was deafening: metal and bricks slamming together with the force of a meteorite; wood and glass splintering, shattering. The entire house around Xander shuddered and let out a sharp groan. Debris pounded against the shield like three men beating at it with sledgehammers. Xander held firm, pulled himself into a tighter ball behind it. He felt a sharp crack on the back of his head, and a broken brick fell to the floor.

Little bits of wall—plaster, brick, wood—rained down on him. A thick cloud of dust swirled into his space—over, under, around the shield. It swept into his mouth, down into his lungs. He coughed, hacking it out.

He stood, fanning at the cloud in front of his face. Sunlight streamed in, making the dust glow and appear that much more impenetrable. He held the shield up and swung it out and back, out and back, hoping to clobber Taksidian if the man moved in to finish off his prey.

Xander coughed. "Dad?" he said. "Dad?"

The cloud thinned, revealing the crumpled front of the Bug. The car was more in the room than out of it. Only its back wheels and stubby rear end hadn't entered. A huge hole in the house gaped like the mouth of a cave. Layers of house lined the edges: two-by-four studs, puffy pink insulation, bricks. The damage formed an uneven semicircle around the Bug. The top of this arch reached as high as the ceiling, which had buckled and cracked. A brick fell, bounced off the exposed concrete foundation, and rolled into the yard. Another dropped, landing with a thunk on the roof of the car.

Among the debris on the hood was the woolen shirt from the soldier's uniform. It was sprawled over the accordioned hood, arms out, as though a pedestrian had been knocked right out of his clothes. The windshield was shattered so completely,

Xander could not see through it. The car's engine continued to race, seeming to Xander like a movie soundtrack designed to accompany a tense scene in which the hero gets attacked.

He snapped his gaze around the room. Taksidian was gone. He checked the floor, hoping to see his body. Bricks and plaster, weapons and artifacts, glass and severed limbs were scattered everywhere, but no bad guy.

Crunching over the rubble, he moved to the VW's side window and peered inside. The view was fragmented by the shattered glass, but painfully clear: Dad was slumped forward in the seat, his head pressing against the top of the steering wheel. While Xander watched, a thick rivulet of blood appeared from under his father's head and ran down the arc of the wheel.

# CHAPTER

# five

Keal hammered against an old, splintered board until it came away from the nails that had held it to the ceiling for who-knew-how-long and fell to the floor. He backed down a stepladder to appraise the area that was now ready for new wood.

When he had come to the house—tagging along as Jesse's nurse—he could never have guessed what he was getting himself into. Time travel. A kidnapped mom. Vicious brutes, out to kill little kids.

He turned to glance at Toria, only nine and already more familiar with danger and grief than Keal was. She was sitting on the floor at the junction of the second-floor hallways, doing what she called homework, but it looked to Keal like she was coloring a drawing of the house. She looked up at him and smiled.

*Who'd want to hurt such sweetness?* Keal thought, winking at her. He had known the King kids only a few days, but already felt something for them that might have been love. Maybe it was the intensity of the experiences they had shared: battling Phemus, finding the future ruins of Los Angeles, saving Nana from getting pulled back into history. Maybe it was that they seemed like good people, and bad things—*very* bad things—were happening to them. All he knew for sure was that he wanted to protect them, to use his training as a former Army Ranger to show them how to fight, help them get their mother back, and prevent more harm from befalling them.

He closed his eyes. In *this* house, that wouldn't be easy. Wasn't he supposed to have kept Jesse safe? And look what had happened to him: stabbed and in the hospital at that very moment, maybe recovering, maybe not. He vowed to do a better job with the Kings.

He returned his attention to the task at hand. He was working on the walls Phemus had knocked down the day before.

Before that destructive attempt to get Xander, David, and Toria, the walls had been positioned at the bottom of the staircase that ascended to the third-floor hallway of doors. There had been two walls: the one closest to the stairs had boasted a metal-fortified but ultimately pointless door; the second one, six feet from the first, had been disguised to look like the end of the short hallway, which ran toward the back of the house from the main second-floor hallway. Pushing in just the right spot had caused a secret door to pop open.

Keal understood the logic that had gone into such a configuration. The secret door would not have been very secret if it flaunted hasps and locks and deadbolts. But because bad people came out of the portal doors upstairs, security was essential. That's where the other wall and door came in.

And who knew? Maybe it had worked in the past, keeping all manner of time travelers out of the house. It just hadn't worked yesterday. For whatever reason—probably a stern order from Taksidian—Phemus hadn't let it deter him from his mission of getting the kids. From what Xander had told Keal about the attack, the wall had slowed down their attackers long enough to let the children escape, so it had done some good.

Keal had decided to reconstruct the walls pretty much the way they had been, with one difference: he planned to make both walls extra sturdy, and he would find a way to make the inner door *impossible* to break through.

Earlier in the afternoon, Ed King had called to say he and

the boys were going on a "mission," and would Keal mind picking up Toria from her elementary school? Afterward, Keal and Toria had stopped by the lumber store for the items they would need to make the house right again.

Thinking about it now, Keal laughed.

"What's funny?" Toria said.

"Ah, nothing," he said. "I was just thinking that putting these walls up was making the house right . . . but how can this house ever be *right?*"

Toria pressed her lips together and furrowed her brow. She said, "I know what Xander would say. He'd say the house will be right when we rescue Mom and get out of it. For good."

Keal nodded. "I like that idea."

Worded that simply, their task in the house sounded easy. But he knew that finding Mrs. King meant going in and out of different times in history—times that seemed always to be full of life-threatening dangers. Even if—yes, that was the word, he thought glumly: *if*—they were able to rescue her, they couldn't just leave. They had found out that the future of mankind was no future at all. Sometime soon, there would be a war that wiped out Los Angeles—Keal had seen the ruins himself—and presumably the rest of the world. Jesse thought there was something they could do to fix things; in fact, he had said it was their *duty* to change the future. It was hard for Keal to disagree: if there was something they could do, they had to try to do it.

Toria was watching his face as he thought all of this, obviously not liking what she saw. He forced a smile and said, "That'll be a great day, huh? Saying adios to this crazy place once and for all."

She grinned and returned to her drawing, adding a tree trunk beside the gray house. His heart ached for her, a sweet little girl who'd experienced more trauma, grief, and frights than any kid should have to face.

He noticed a few nails protruding from the ceiling and climbed the ladder to pound them in.

"More hammering?" Toria complained.

"'Fraid so." He glanced over his shoulder at her. She had a hand pressed over each ear. Loudly, he said, "Maybe you should do that in your room."

She shook her head.

Keal shrugged, angled his arm to strike the nails, and stopped. He looked back at Toria again. Hands still in place to ease the sound of his pounding, she was looking down at her drawing. Her long, dark hair hung all the way to the page.

"What did you say?" he called.

She looked up, removed her hands. "What?"

"Did you say something?"

"When?"

"Just now." He was sure he had heard something. He listened.

"What?" she said.

"Shhh," he said. "Thought I heard—there!"

"I don't hear anything," she said.

He held his hand up to silence her.

There it was again: a quiet, sustained *scream.* Toria's eyes widened.

"See?" he said.

She nodded slowly. Her eyes slid to their right edges as she listened. "Somebody's screaming!" she said, hopping up. She ran into the main hall, out of his sight.

"Hey," he said. "Wait!"

But she had already hit the stairs, heading to the first floor.

Keal jumped off the ladder and swerved around the corner. He was on the stairs when she opened the front door and disappeared. He found her on the porch, her head cocked sideways.

"Can't hear it out here," she whispered. She came back to the foyer.

Keal stepped in and shut the door. Immediately the scream reached his ears, still muffled—as though from a great distance—but louder and clearer. It was hideous, a screech of such pain and rage, it made him think of a banshee, the mythical spirit that came for the souls of the dying. He felt a cold shiver shoot up his spine.

Toria swung her face toward him. Her eyes were wide and scared. She said, "I know what it is!"

CHAPTER

# Six

THURSDAY, 6:37 P.M.

Dad wasn't moving. Through the shattered glass, Xander couldn't tell if he was even breathing.

But he *was* bleeding.

He pounded his palm against the window. "Dad!" He tried the door handle. The button depressed, but the door wouldn't budge. It was crinkled and appeared to be pushed back into the metal behind it.

Xander ran around the front to the driver's side. Dad was still in the same position, his head leaning forward onto the wheel, but Xander noticed movement: a blink. Then another.

He rapped on the glass. "Dad!"

Dad lifted his head. He touched his head, winced, looked at his bloody finger. He peered out the window at Xander.

Xander tried to open the door, but that one was jammed shut as well. He yelled through the glass, "Are you all right?"

Dad rubbed his forehead, smearing blood. He nodded. He glanced around, as if trying to find his bearings. He fumbled with the ignition key and turned off the engine.

"Is there danger?" he said, just loud enough for Xander to hear. "Where's Taksidian?"

"I don't know," Xander said, looking toward the door. "I think he left, but he could be waiting to ambush us. He—" Xander hitched in a breath, surprised by the realization he was on the brink of tears. He didn't know if he wanted to cry because he had been so scared, so certain he was going to die, or because he *hadn't* died. Maybe it was seeing Dad like that. Then he decided it was all of the above.

Dad tried the door: no go. He unsnapped his seat belt and thumped his shoulder against the door: it didn't budge.

"The other side's the same," Xander said.

Dad smeared blood out of his right eye socket, then his left. He leaned back, pulled his legs up from the footwell, and kicked at the windshield. It rattled, bulged, but held firm. He kicked again. Little rectangles of glass *tink*ed against sheet metal, then the windshield levered out, flopping onto the hood like the discarded hide of a crystal alligator.

Dad pulled his upper body out through the opening, turned, and sat on the hood. He said, "Taksidian's gone?"

"I think so," Xander said. "He wanted to kill me. He was so casual about it, like it was no big deal."

Dad tugged his shirt up, wiped his eyes, and dabbed at his forehead. When his face was exposed again, Xander saw that the gash traveled from one temple to the other. It arced across his forehead, matching the arc of the steering wheel perfectly.

"Are you all right?" Xander asked again.

"Yeah." Dad's head swiveled to take in the room. "Where's David?"

"I don't know. We have to find him," Xander said.

"Find him? Where—?" He hopped to the floor.

"We got separated when Taksidian came home," Xander said. "I think he went through the window and ran away. I—" He turned toward the room's open door and yelled, "David!"

They were quiet for a few seconds. Xander held his breath, wanting so badly to hear his brother's voice. Not hearing it felt like being underwater, needing to breathe, and knowing the surface was way, way above him. He looked to his father, hoping for reassurance, but he saw only worry.

Xander said, "Maybe he's in the forest."

Dad frowned and yelled, "David!" He headed for the door,

then stopped and returned to Xander. He put his hand on Xander's cheek. "You okay?" Without waiting for an answer, he pulled him in and hugged him. When he let go, he said, "Let's find him." His gaze bore into Xander's eyes. "Quickly, in case he *didn't* get away."

Outside, a car started up.

"Taksidian," Dad said. He moved toward the partially disintegrated outer wall. His foot came down on something that moved under it. He flew back, arms flailing, and Xander caught him. The Mercedes reversed off the pad in front of the garage, braked, and whipped forward down the dirt-road drive.

"He might have Dae!" Dad said. He pushed off Xander and squeezed between the Bug and the broken wall. He ran across the yard and stopped. The Mercedes was already at the first bend, a good hundred yards away. It turned and was gone. Dad tossed up his hands. He turned, his eyes dancing over the house, the woods around it. He made a megaphone out of his hands and yelled, "David!" He waited, listening, then called again.

As Dad strode back to the shattered wall and squeezed through, Xander called for David in the house.

"He'd answer if he was inside," Xander said, keeping his eyes on the open bedroom door. "I don't think Taksidian got him. He didn't have time."

When his father didn't respond, Xander turned.

Dad was staring at the thing he'd stepped on: a severed leg, white and oozing. His gaze darted from it to an arm . . . another leg . . . He covered his mouth with his hand. "What—?" he said, the word coming out muffled.

Xander said, "Taksidian had them stacked up, like some kind of art. I found . . ." He looked for the metal table, saw it twisted against the opposite wall. "I think I found Jesse's finger."

Dad's eyes widened. He went back through the opening, turned toward the garage, and started calling for David. His voice was panicked now, high pitched and frantic.

Xander felt an icy finger touch his heart. What if he was wrong? What if Taksidian *did* have David? The thought of his brother with the man who killed people and took parts from them drove him through the wall opening so fast, he knocked his head on a protruding brick and scraped his shoulder on a broken stud.

He went the other direction, passing the front door and bay window, yelling . . . *screaming* for David.

# CHAPTER

# Seven

David now understood what it meant to scream your head off.
His brain was throbbing; his throat felt like he'd swallowed
glass. He had stopped pounding on the wall when his hand
started bleeding. Of course, he hadn't seen the blood, but the
pain told him he'd done some damage, and when a splatter
struck his face, he had licked his hand and tasted blood.

He let loose with one more ear-piercing holler. It echoed

around the chamber, as they all had. He stumbled back and sat hard on the ground—on the *bones*. He didn't care anymore. He was too tired, too scared, too sore in too many places. He dropped his face into his cupped hands and began crying, loud, uncontrollable sobs.

The darkness spoke his name.

He tried to stop bawling, but he couldn't. He lifted his head, breathed wet sobs into the air. He prayed he would not hear his name again, mumbled perhaps by the ghosts of the people who had already died in the room. Or worse: he had imagined it. The darkness and fear were getting to him. He was losing it. And if he could hallucinate his name, then he could hallucinate *anything*: grabbing hands, monsters, whole skeletons reassembled from the broken bones around him.

He dropped his face into his hands again, shook it back and forth.

*No! No! No!*

The chamber was bad enough as it was. He couldn't share it with monsters, even if they *were* only tricks created by his own mind. What did it matter if they were real or imagined? They could still get him. His craziness would get so bad, he would probably start scratching at himself, believing his hands were some other creature's talons.

He cried harder.

After everything he'd gone through, all the things he thought he *might* go through looking for Mom, of course he had pondered the possibility of his own death. Stabbed/shot/ blown up by some soldier who mistook him for the enemy. Eaten by creatures who had been extinct for a million years. Portaling into some natural disaster. He knew there were a thousand ways to die—but like *this*? Alone in some nothing room? He wouldn't even know when in history or where in the world he had died until his spirit drifted up out of his dead body and finally out of here, *way* out of here. *Come on!*

He supposed if he didn't gouge out his own eyes or do something else completely insane, then it would be starvation that would get him. Now that was a death he had never considered. He'd been hungry, *really* hungry, a time or two. But there had always been a Snickers or a sandwich or something nearby. He doubted he had ever actually been starving, but he sure didn't like the pain in his stomach when he needed to eat. He imagined that pain doubled, tripled . . . What a terrible way to go. Would he resort to eating his own foot, pretending it was a hamburger? He'd read a short story about a guy who did that. The need to eat was that bad.

*Stop it!* he told himself. *You're not there yet, not even close.*

He remembered not eating his lunch at school.

*Stupid. Should have eaten something, even that nasty pizza I gave Marcus or that slop that was probably rice pudding.*

*Stop!*

He concentrated on crying, just crying. He listened to himself, and felt glad for the distraction from his thoughts.

Again the darkness whispered his name. "David . . ."

He stopped sobbing and tried to listen over his jittery breathing.

"David?"

He scrambled to his feet and slapped the wall. "Here! I'm here! Help!"

Something rapped against stone—behind him. He spun, staring into the blackness. It came again: *Rap! Rap!*

He stepped across to the wall, pounded on it. "I hear you! I'm here! Please!"

"David! What are you doing in there?"

It was Keal. He recognized the deep voice.

"How'd you get in there?" the man yelled, and struck the wall with something. *Rap!* "Can you get out?"

David laughed. He laughed so hard, a stitch of pain poked his side. He bent over, his palm on the wall, still laughing. "No!" he yelled. "I'm stuck."

Another voice called through, quieter, daintier—Toria: "Are you all right, Dae?"

"I am now! Get me out of here!"

# eight

THURSDAY, 6:46 P.M.

Xander returned to the front of the house and joined Dad, and together they called for David.

Dad stopped at a spigot and cranked on the water. He splashed his face, spending extra time on his forehead. He pulled off his sport coat and dried himself. He pressed a sleeve against his forehead and started for the woods, aiming for the spot where the three of them had hidden earlier to watch the house. He yelled David's name.

He had just pushed through the bushes when his phone began chirping. The sound came from the house.

"Dad," Xander yelled. "Your phone's ringing. Where is it?"

Dad appeared puzzled for a moment. He said, "The car."

Xander started for it, then stopped. "Dad," he said, "Taksidian has been bugging our phones."

"What?"

"That's how he knew we were following him." Xander's face tightened. "It's how he was able to set us up, to get David and me alone."

"It could be Taksidian calling," Dad said, pointing at the VW. "Maybe he does have David."

Xander hurried through the opening in the wall. He climbed onto the hood, crawled over the collapsed windshield, and slipped through the opening. He followed the chirping to the passenger footwell, where he pushed aside a pile of garbage and snatched up the phone.

"Hello?"

"David's here," the deep voice rumbled through the tiny speaker.

Taksidian! Xander's breath stuck in his throat.

"Xander, that you? You hear me?" Taksidian said, but then Xander realized his mistake.

"*Keal?*"

"Yes! David's here, in the house. I thought he was with you."

"He was," Xander said. "But—" His mind couldn't get a grip on the idea that David was home. If Keal had said that Toria had turned into a pterodactyl and flown away, Xander wouldn't have been more baffled. Their home was a couple of miles east of town; Taksidian's, a couple of miles *west* of town— an hour's walk, at least. But barely twenty minutes had passed since Taksidian came home and the boys scrambled to hide.

An image came to mind, and Xander smiled: David so scared by Taksidian, his legs became pinwheels that carried him home so fast he left a path of burning footprints behind him. Road-runner in blue jeans and Reeboks. At heart, though, Xander didn't care *how* David had gotten away, only that he had.

Keal spoke away from the phone: "Toria, get back up here. He can't hear you, sweetie. We'll go back down in a minute."

Dad stomped over the debris beside the car. "Keal, hold on," Xander said into the phone. Through the shattered glass of a side window, his father looked like a photograph that had been cut into strips and glued imperfectly back together. Xander tapped the phone against the window. "Dad! David's home!"

Ten years fell away from his father's face as his expression shifted instantly from worry to joy. "How?" He stumbled toward the windshield opening.

"How?" Xander repeated into the phone. "How'd he get there?"

"That's what I was going to ask you," Keal said. "But what's weird is—"

"Xander," Dad said. He was reaching into the car. "Let me talk to him."

Xander handed him the phone. "It's Keal."

"Keal, put David on," Dad said. "Please." As he listened, his forehead became more and more wrinkled. The cut, which was starting to scab, drizzled out two fresh threads of blood. He lifted his coat to dab at them. Finally he said, "He's all right? You're sure?"

"What is it?" Xander said. "What happened?"

Dad said into the phone, "Uh . . . there's a pile of old tools out back, next to the porch steps. There might be a sledge-hammer."

"A sledgehammer?" Xander said, pushing himself up out of the car. "Why—"

But Dad turned around and took a step away. He said, "Okay, we'll get there as soon as we can. Call us if . . . call us *when* you get him out." He punched a button and dropped the phone into his shirt pocket. He turned around slowly, thinking.

"Well?" Xander said, going nuts. "What happened? Where is he? Why do they need a sledgehammer? Get him out of *where?*"

"David's in the basement," Dad said. "Keal heard scream-ing and followed it. David's stuck behind a wall. Come on, we have to get back . . . make sure he gets out . . . make sure he's not hurt." He slipped outside.

"A wall?" Xander said. "Wait. How?"

Dad was speedwalking out of the yard and onto the drive.

"Hey," Xander said, "call my phone!"

"Hurry, Xander!" Dad said without looking back.

*A Fistful of Dollars* started up. Xander located the phone among the rubble, resting in the palm of one of Taksidian's trophies. He picked it up, scrubbed it against his jeans, and shoved it into his back pocket. He took a last look around: at the body parts, the demolished wall, the totaled car—the car! Dan, the kid who had lent it to him, was going to kill him.

As he slipped outside and started jogging toward Dad, he reconsidered his choice of words. *Taksidian* was going to kill him, if he had his way. Dan was just going to make Xander *wish* he were dead.

# CHAPTER

# nine

Keal levered the sledgehammer behind him, remembering his days as a slugger in college. His eyes found Toria, back against another wall in the dim basement. She was aiming a flashlight at the wall in front of Keal. "Watch out," he told her.

Toria nodded.

"Ready, David?" he yelled.

"Hold on!" came the boy's voice through the wall. It was

muted, as though he had spoken into a pillow. "I'm lighting a match. . . . Okay, do it!"

"Cover your head!" Keal said. He put everything he had into the swing. The hammer struck the gray stone wall with a resounding *bam!* and an eruption of sparks. The energy of the strike vibrated up the handle into his arms. He kept hold of the handle, but let the hammer's head drop to the floor. The fuzzy-edged glow of the flashlight illuminated a small gash in the stone, light gray against the surrounding dark gray. The stone he had struck was still perfectly aligned with the others around it.

Keal called, "Anything on your side, David?"

"A loud noise!"

*Okay*, he thought, sighing. *This is going to take awhile.*

He lifted the hammer, pulled it back, swung it hard.

•••••••• ••

David smiled. He held a lit match in one hand and pressed the other hand against the wall. He felt the thuds of Keal's sledgehammer coming through the wall like a heartbeat. They meant more to him than Keal's and Toria's voices had. Voices he could hallucinate, but he didn't think he'd imagine anything as physical as a trembling wall. Not this early anyway; maybe eventually, but it seemed now he'd never know.

And that's what made him smile.

43

The match's flame singed his skin. He dropped it and stuck his finger and thumb in his mouth. The fire had left a glowing yellow spot in his vision, fading slowly, leaving only the black air of the chamber.

Didn't matter now. He was being rescued.

He wondered how Mom felt: like she was stuck without hope, or as though she were being rescued? She had to know they were looking for her, had to know they wouldn't stop until they found her. So, really, even though she had no evidence of it—unless she'd seen the Bob cartoon face, their family symbol, that they'd left in each world—she had to know her rescue was in progress. He hoped she knew that, and that it comforted her. Wouldn't a person lost in the wilderness feel better, keep his hopes up longer, if he saw the helicopter that was looking for him? The Kings were that helicopter for Mom, and they would never run out of fuel, be grounded by bad weather, or say they'd looked too long. They would never give up.

He stepped back away from the pounding and leaned against the opposite wall. He didn't bother lighting another match. Hearing was enough.

*Bam! Bam!*

*Bam! Bam!*

Like a heart, beating just for him.

# CHAPTER

ten

Xander and Dad walked side-by-side along the winding road leading to Pinedale. Their pace had slowed considerably, but it remained a few notches above a leisurely stroll.

Behind them, the sound of an engine and the low, flat hum of tires on asphalt approached. They stepped off the road into long grass. The dirt here was rutted and uneven, making a chore even out of standing. Trees pressed in so close to the blacktop, Xander had to prop himself against one just to give Dad room to get off the road.

Dad waited until a white pickup truck appeared around a bend, then he stuck out his thumb. He said, "Don't *ever* hitch-hike, you hear?"

"I know," Xander said. "You already said. Just this once, 'cause it's an emergency."

The truck zoomed by without slowing.

"Dad," Xander said, pushing off the tree. "Why is it an emergency?"

Dad got his feet on the road and reached back to give Xander a hand. "Just what Keal said. He hadn't seen David, only heard him. And he'd been screaming."

"Screaming?" Xander said.

"I think for help, not in pain."

Xander shook his head. Who could tell in *that* house? The way it manipulated sounds, you couldn't believe anything you heard. He wouldn't think David was safe until his brother was standing in front of him. Besides, *behind a wall?* What was that about? What else might be behind the wall *with* him? And could whatever put him there, take him back? Where would David go if it did?

Too many questions—as usual. Since moving in, they'd been dealing with weirdness with a capital W: traveling through space and time, maniacs bent on killing them, history that *changed* based on what they did in the other worlds. Jesse had said David made the world different when he saved a little girl in World War II. She had grown up to help cure smallpox. Before he'd saved her, the disease had been killing millions of people every year. Then, twenty minutes after Dae jumped through a portal, thinking he'd seen Mom, the whole world was different; the disease was gone, eradicated thirty years before.

It seemed the more they found out about the house, the more they didn't know. Every answer led to a dozen more questions. The biggest mystery was how any of them was still sane.

They started walking again, and Dad put his hand on the back of Xander's head, pushing his fingers through his hair. Xander flinched, pulling his head away. Dad's hand came back bloody.

"Xander?" Dad said, looking from his fingers to Xander's head.

Xander touched the spot where the brick had conked him. "It's nothing," he said. "Headache's all. I think it just opened up the cut I got when the wall light landed on my head. You know, when we were trying to stop Phemus from taking Mom. If it's a new cut, I better not ever go bald. My scars will scare children."

Dad eyed him, uncertain. Finally he offered a faint smile. "Shakespeare said, 'A scar nobly got is honorable.'" He shrugged. "Something like that."

Xander rubbed his head. "I say, a scar nobly got *hurts*."

# CHAPTER

# eleven

Keal kept pummeling the same square stone. Little chips in the shape of tiny smiles eventually became a fist-sized indent. Finally a crack appeared, running from the hammer's damage to a corner.

Keal leaned in. He ran a palm over his eyes, brow, and head, squeegeeing away beads of sweat.

"It's giving up," he said. He had begun to think of the wall as an opponent. It was strong and stubborn, but so was he. He looked back at Toria with a winning grin. "First a crack, then a stone, then the whole wall, right?"

"It cracked, Dae!" she yelled.

His muffled voice came back: "Yah!"

Keal hefted the hammer, reared back, and slammed it into the stone. He did it again and again, without pause. His breathing fell in sync with his efforts: a sharp inhale as he pulled back, a loud grunt on the forward swing. Sweat flew off his head, sparkling in the flashlight's beam.

The stone crumbled, dust and chunks spilling to the floor.

Toria rushed in to light the gap. Eight inches in, another stone showed its flat, resilient face. The wall was at least two blocks thick. She moaned.

"No, no," Keal said. "It'll be easy now. Once you get one block out of a wall like this, the others have room to shift. They'll start falling away in no time. You'll see."

He was right: the block above its crumbled neighbor chipped, broke, and fell away after only four strikes. When the first layer's opening was four blocks wide and four blocks tall—a square about the size of a television screen—Keal started pounding on the second layer.

"Dust!" David said, no longer sounding like he was talking into a pillow. "And that was loud, really loud."

"Cover up," Keal yelled back, taking aim. "For real this time."

Three more hits and a block pushed in, three inches from the surface of the blocks on either side of it.

"I felt it!" David screamed. "It moved."

"Back away, David!"

The next strike sent it sailing into the darkness behind it.

"Ow!" David said. Then: "Let there be light!"

Toria charged up to the wall. The flashlight beam wavered around the square hole and slipped into the blackness beyond. David's face appeared, smiling, squinting against the brightness. He laughed.

"Dae!" Toria chimed.

"Where are we?" David said.

Keal and Toria looked at each other. Keal said, "You're home, son. In the house."

"The basement," Toria added.

David closed his eyes. "I should have known." His lids flipped opened and looked past Toria at the walls and exposed trusses. "I thought I was back in time somewhere—but how could that happen from Taksidian's house? It's just that I found the other side first. Like if we'd discovered the locker–linen closet portal from the locker side. It's still not the locker doing it, it's the house. It's always the house."

"What are you talking about?" Toria said. "How'd you get in there?"

"I'll explain later," he said. His eyes found Keal. "Just get me out . . . *please*."

"What's in there?" Keal asked.

"Nothing. *Bones.*"

"Bones?" Toria said.

"Human bones," David continued. "Skeletons. But most of them are broken up, ground down to nothing. Gravel."

"Eeeew!"

"I thought for sure," David said, "that my bones would wind up in here too, lying on top until someone else got trapped and tromped me into dust."

Toria touched her fingers to his cheek. He reached his hand out, and she took it.

"Okay," Keal said. "Back off. We'll have your bones out of there in a flash." He lifted the hammer.

The kids released their hands, and David's disappeared into the hole. Toria stuck her face up to it. "Hey, Dae," she said, "wouldn't that be funny to find a skeleton with a cast on its arm?"

"Not if it's me," David said.

Toria giggled, then took her spot behind Keal.

He hauled back on the sledgehammer and let it fly, enjoying every sweaty blow. He took great satisfaction not only in rescuing David but in destroying the thing that held him captive. It felt like springing an innocent man from his cell, then burning down the jail.

He pounded on the first layer below and to the sides of the hole, stretching it out so he could get better shots at the second layer. A mound of broken stones formed on the floor.

He stopped and said, "David, I'm ready to knock the cubes out on your side of the wall. Ready?"

"Ready to get out of here."

"Get in the corner closest to me," Keal instructed. "The stone will fly back away from you." He heard crunching from within, pictured the bones David was walking over. *Man!*

"Ready," David said.

Keal beat the wall down, chunk by chunk, stone by stone. He heard the pieces striking a wall inside and only then realized how tight the space was in there. He grunted and yelled, taking his anger out on the blasted wall.

"Okay . . . okay!" David yelled.

Keal realized the boy had been calling out for some time. He dropped the sledgehammer and leaned over, propping his arms on his knees. He panted and watched sweat drop from his face to the floor.

David appeared in the opening, Toria's light gliding over him. Gray dust coated his hair, face, and clothes.

"Tell me that's wall dust!" Toria said. "And not *people* dust."

David brushed it off his cheek, coughed, and patted his chest, kicking up another plume. He said, "A little of both, I think."

"Let's get you out of there," Keal said, reaching out for him.

As David stepped over the wall, he lost his balance and fell back into the chamber. On his way, he grabbed at the side of the opening, dislodging a stone, which dislodged the one above it. The block above that one gave way as well, then an entire column of blocks came down, one at a time, faster and faster.

"Look out!" Keal said, pushing Toria with his arm. "David, get back!"

"I'm—" David started. Any words that followed reached Keal's ears sounding like a howling wind.

Toria's light caught David in the act of lifting himself off the chamber floor . . . or still falling onto it. He seemed to be hovering above it, his arms rotating for balance, one foot kicking in the air. His T-shirt fluttered and rippled, as though wind were billowing under it. Beyond his chest, David's face was white and wide-eyed. His mouth moved, a silent scream for help. The blackness around him moved in, seeming to flow over him like liquid—

*Or a hand,* Keal thought. He could almost see thick, black fingers slipping around David.

Then he was gone.

Toria's light played on the far wall and floor of the empty chamber. She cried out her brother's name.

# CHAPTER

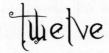

twelve

David crashed down on a hard surface. The light was dim, seeping into the area he occupied only from around a narrow door on his right. But he could make out shelves above him. They were lined with cans, plastic-wrapped loaves of bread, a bag of chips.

*Taksidian's pantry!* he realized. *I came back.*

Still moving, either from the teleportation itself or from

his own jostling around as he tried to get his balance, he spun on his tailbone. His foot hit the center of the bifold door. It slid open. Sunlight streamed in. He blinked, squinted . . . and gasped in terror.

Taksidian was staring at him. Standing in the kitchen, he was bent over a big black trash bag, tying a knot in the top. His face was turned toward the pantry, and he seemed as startled to see David as David was to see him.

The man said, "Boy!" and sprang for him. His arms reached, his hands stretched out. His nails appeared impossibly long, impossibly sharp.

David grabbed the edge of the door and pulled it closed— or he would have if his foot wasn't still positioned dead center with the door, keeping it from popping shut. He pulled his foot back.

Taksidian's fingers circled around the edge of the door.

David felt the door slipping away from his grasp. He tightened his grip and pulled. Before Taksidian could get his other hand on the edge and yank with the power of both arms, David did the first thing that came to his mind. He shifted his legs under him, rose to his knees, and sank his teeth into Taksidian's fingers.

The man howled. David opened his mouth, and the fingers flashed away through the opening. He yanked at the door, closing it.

A warm, scentless breath came up from the floor, down from

above, circling around from the sides of the pantry, washing over him. Darkness came with it. The floor under his knees vaporized. For an instant, he felt as though he'd been dropped off a cliff. Then solid ground formed under him. Not so solid, actually: it was the gravelly bones of the chamber. They crunched beneath him.

"David!" Toria yelled.

The flashlight beam shined in his face.

"What just happened?" Keal said.

David sprang up and reached for the man. "Get me outta here!" he said. "Don't let me fall back!"

Keal grabbed him and began hoisting him through the opening.

Wind swirled behind David, whipping through the hair on the back of his head, fluttering his shirt. He glanced back and saw what he had only imagined earlier: a vampire, its face and hands ghostly white drifting out of the darkness toward him. But it wasn't a vampire—

"Taksidian!" David screamed, scrambling to get his legs over the wall, clawing at Keal's shoulders to pull himself out.

Hands clasped over his ankles, yanking him back a few inches.

"Hey!" Keal yelled. Squeezing David tighter, he threw himself backward.

David felt like the rope in a tug-o'-war. Then his feet slipped through Taksidian's grip, and he flew through the opening. He felt long, bony fingers on his calves, squirming over them, trying to sink into them. David pulled his legs up, felt the fingers slide over his ankles and heels, snag the top of his sneaker, and slip away. He fell on top of Keal, who landed hard on his back.

Keal tossed him aside. David rolled, looking back to see Taksidian half out of the opening, his body bent over the remaining wall. He was still reaching, clawing for David. The man snapped his twisted face toward Keal. Taksidian's eyes flashed wide, then narrowed into a squinty glare. He looked between David and Keal, as though figuring out whether he could still get David, determined to do it regardless of anything else.

Keal leapt up, the sledgehammer miraculously in his hands. He hoisted it back.

Taksidian jerked sideways. The hammer struck the blocks beside him, kicking up sparks and dust. Keal pulled the hammer back. As he swung it, Taksidian pushed off the wall, back into the chamber. The hammer cracked against the wall. A block disappeared into the blackness beyond. Keal hefted the hammer back again and waited. He reversed a step.

"Come out of there!" he yelled. "Hands first! Show me your hands."

Nothing. Not a sound. No movement.

Keal waited. Finally, he said, "David . . . ?"

"I got it," David said. He rose and took the flashlight from Toria. Shining it into the opening, he stepped closer.

"Careful," Keal said.

One more step, then up on his tiptoes. He raised the light, moved the beam around through the opening. "He's gone," David said.

"Maybe," Keal said. "Maybe not."

David moved closer. "I can see the back wall and the floor."

"Okay, come here." Keal held the sledgehammer out to him. "Trade with me."

The hammer was heavier than it looked, and it looked heavy. David pushed it up over his head, as though it were a barbell. "Okay."

Keal leaned into the opening, aimed the light at the ground nearest them.

"What?" Toria said.

"Nothing. He's gone."

David dropped the hammer. It clattered to the floor, and he fell onto his hands and knees beside it. He spat on the floor. Spat again. He felt Keal's hand on his back.

"David?" Keal said.

Holding his head low, he raised an index finger: *Give me a minute.* He could taste Taksidian's blood on his tongue. He retched, opened his mouth to puke, but nothing came up. He spat and watched a string of drool dangle from his lip to the floor. He leaned back and sat on his heels. He wiped his mouth on the back of his hand, saw blood smeared with slobber, and rubbed it off on his jeans.

"I didn't think going through a portal could make you sick," Keal said. "Tired, but not sick."

"I bit him," David said.

"You what?"

"I had to," David said. "I went back to his house. He saw me, tried to grab me. I had to bite him to get away." David spat again. "Tasted like raw steak. *Old* steak."

"Gross!" Toria declared.

David looked around Keal at the broken wall. He said, "He might come back."

Toria backed away.

Keal handed the flashlight to her and scooped up the sledgehammer. He stood in front of the opening, legs apart, hammer cocked over his shoulder, and said, "Let him come."

CHAPTER

THURSDAY, 7:07 P.M.

The circle of light from Toria's flashlight trembled over the edges of the ragged opening. It slipped into the chamber and wobbled against the far wall. It skimmed over Keal's back, casting a giant shadow of their protector on the wall.

David pulled his legs out from under him and sat on the floor.

They waited like that for a few minutes. Finally, Keal glanced around the basement, which was lit by weak, yellowish bulbs mounted to ceiling trusses here and there. A labyrinth of walls divided the area into rooms. From any given spot, not much of the basement was visible.

"Anything we can use to block this thing?" he said.

David tried to remember. He'd been down here only once, when he, Xander, and Dad had inspected the basement, looking for ways someone could get into the house. Or for "squatters," as Dad had referred to people living where they didn't belong. David had thought it was a funny word and didn't even want to know what someone would be doing *squatting* in their basement. Now he wished they *had* found people living down here, to explain the big bare footprints Mom had seen in the dust on the dining room floor. That would have been much better than the truth, that some bad guy was coming into their house from the past.

"I can't remember," he said.

Keal backed away from the opening. He set the head of the sledgehammer on the floor next to David's knee. Its handle rose straight up.

Keal said, "Toria, wait here with your brother. I need your flashlight for a few minutes."

She handed it to him and dropped down to her knees beside David. She put an arm around his shoulders.

Keal returned to the chamber and leaned into it again, flashing the light around.

"Don't," David said. He felt like a guy who'd been bitten by a lion, only to see his friend stick his head into the beast's mouth.

Keal threw an anxious look at him and stepped away from the hole. "I'll be right back. Holler if you hear or see anything, especially in the chamber."

"You really didn't have to say that," David said.

Keal smiled and walked around a corner. "Keep talking," he called out, "so I know you're safe."

"About what?" Toria said.

"Anything. I just want to hear you."

"La la la la la," Toria said. She smiled at David, then frowned. "What happened?" She was looking at his knuckles, bloody and bruised.

He rubbed them. "Pounding on the wall."

"Does it hurt?"

He shook his head.

She called over her shoulder to Keal. "Shouldn't we call Dad, let him know David's okay?"

"Good idea," Keal answered.

Toria crawled across the floor a short distance and returned with the house's wireless phone. She punched the buttons and said, "We got him. David. He's okay. Well, he almost threw up, but he's okay now."

David shook his head. Sealed up behind a wall. Teleporting away and back again. Taksidian! And it's his almost barfing that Toria tells Dad about. "Let me talk to him." He took the phone from her. "Dad?"

"Are you hurt?"

"No, I'm good. But, Dad, listen. There's another portal. It—"

"Wait," Dad interrupted. "Xander tells me Taksidian's been bugging our phones."

David bit his lip. "I forgot," he whispered.

"Don't say something you don't want him to hear."

"I don't want him to hear anything," David said. He pushed the handle of the sledgehammer. It dipped almost to the floor, then righted itself. He supposed they would have to give up using phones altogether. Strange how their lives were starting to resemble a video game: as soon as you gained one advantage—say, getting Nana back—something happened that cranked up the difficulty level.

"I love you, Dae."

"Love you, Dad."

He disconnected and set the phone on the floor.

Toria studied his face. "Were you crying?"

"Not now," he said. He tapped the hammer's handle again. It dipped and came back up.

"Before?"

"Like a baby," he said, an embarrassed smile creasing his lips. "I kind of thought I was getting tougher. You know, getting used to almost dying about once an hour, but . . ." He looked at the opening and finished his sentence in his head: *Man, that was bad.* He shook his head, perplexed by how quickly he had crumbled. "I wasn't even in there that long."

"The chamber?" Keal said. He was dragging a huge wooden steamer trunk toward the opening. Something in David's expression made him stop. He set the trunk down and sat on it. He said, "Sensory deprivation. It's one of the worst forms of torture. Can't hear, can't see. No contact at all. It usually takes a couple of days for the full effects to kick in, unless—"

"See?" David said, disgusted with himself. "I was flipping out in two minutes."

Keal held up his index finger. "I said *unless.*" He waited until he saw he had David's attention. "Unless you don't know how you got there or how long you'll be there. Most prisoners of war understand the tactic, and they know it won't last forever. Mentally, they're prepared. For them, it's not a matter of being scared, it's . . . something else. But you had no idea where you were. The bones told you other people had died in there. You're a smart kid. You calculated the horror of your situation quickly. Given all that, *of course* it got to you fast. I think you handled yourself better than most people would have." He leaned down and slapped David's knee.

David smiled. "Thanks, Keal."

Keal got to his feet, then tapped David's head. "What say you help me cover this up?" he said, pointing his thumb at the chamber.

"A trunk?" David said. "That's not going to keep anyone out."

"I've got some plywood sheets upstairs," Keal said. "Some two-by-fours and rebar. Everything we need to button this thing up good. But I'm not going to leave you guys down here alone while I get them, and I'm not going to leave that hole the way it is, unattended. Someone could come through and hide in the basement until we leave again."

"Yeah, but . . . the *trunk*?"

"Trust me," Keal said. "Okay?"

They stood the trunk up on its side. It was taller than David. As they scooted it in front of the opening, David caught the backsplash of Toria's light skittering around the walls inside the chamber. His stomach flopped over on itself. The room wasn't a chamber; it was a crypt. For a while, it had been *his* crypt.

The trunk blocked all but thin gaps on the sides and top of the opening. Keal reached into his pocket and pulled out some coins. "Okay, watch," he said. He placed a quarter on the top edge of the trunk, barely hanging over. He did the same with a dime and two pennies. "Now if anyone even nudges it, the coins will fall off, and we'll know someone was here."

"They'll hear them hit the floor," David said. "They'll know what you did and put them back."

"Ah," Keal said. "But I put each one facing a different direction, and only I know exactly how they were placed. Like a combination lock."

David smiled and nodded. "Smart."

Keal gave him a little push. "You thought I *wasn't* smart?"

As they backed away from the chamber toward the stairs, David thought again how much it resembled a crypt. He wondered how much time he had before it wanted him back.

# CHAPTER

# fourteen

Having reached town—cars driving around, people going about their business—Xander and Dad stopped looking over their shoulders for Taksidian every two seconds. They were about to cross a driveway into a business's parking lot when Taksidian's black Mercedes pulled off the main road into the drive and stopped in front of them.

Dad threw his arm across Xander's chest and took a step

back. Their fear was reflected back at them in the car's black-tinted side windows.

Xander swiveled his head, looking to see if Taksidian's accomplices, his henchmen, were moving in on them. The sun cast an orange tinge into the western sky, leaving the rest sapped of color; the twilight left too many shadowy places to hide for Xander to be sure of anything.

He imagined a car full of hulking creatures like the ones who had attacked David, Toria, and him the day before. They would spring out like trapdoor spiders and pull them in. The image gave way to another less dramatic but equally lethal scenario: Taksidian with a silenced pistol.

"Dad?" he said.

"Get ready to run," Dad whispered.

The driver's window slid down, revealing Taksidian's gaunt and supremely smug face. His gaze took in Xander, then moved slowly to Dad. Words rolled out of his mouth like swells on an ocean, deep and smooth: "Join me for a piece of pie?" He nodded at something through the windshield. They were in front of the diner the Kings had eaten at on their second day in Pinedale.

"You tried to kill me!" Xander said, straining against Dad's arm. "And my brother! You stabbed Jesse, took his finger! You kidnapped my mother!"

Taksidian pursed his lips and swirled his hand in the air, as if to say, *I know, I know . . . get it all out, if it makes you feel better.*

"Xander," Dad said. He turned his back to Taksidian and placed a firm hand on Xander's chest. "Not here."

Xander snapped his face toward his father, the blazing hatred for Taksidian now directed at him. "What's with you?" he said. "How can you *not* want to tear him apart? Who else has to be kidnapped, who has to die before you do something?"

Taksidian watched them with those bored eyes—but Xander knew they were *alert* eyes. His high forehead and long kinky hair reminded Xander of the creepy undertaker in the movie *Phantasm*.

Taksidian shook his head. With the precision of a skilled actor, he managed to focus whole soliloquies of contempt and disdain into a single word: "Teenagers."

Dad's muscles tightened, but he ignored the man. He hooked his fingers around Xander's bicep and said, "Come with me." He led Xander away from the car.

"I don't get you," Xander said. "You know what he's done!"

"I know what our goals are," Dad said. "Do I *want* to tear him apart? I do. Is it the best way to get your mother back? I don't think so. He may be the only person who *can* bring her back to us."

"Him?" Xander said. "*We* can find her!"

"I think we can too," Dad said. "But let's find out what he wants. Maybe we'll learn something that'll help us."

Xander glared past Dad at Taksidian's profile. The man was staring through his windshield, drumming his fingernails against the steering wheel. Xander shook his head. "He wants to have *pie* with us? Come on!"

Dad whispered, "He wants to make sure we're not going to the cops. There's a lot of evidence back at his house. I'll bet those body parts can be traced back to, I don't know, missing people . . . murders."

"Then let's do it," Xander said. "Let's turn him in."

"Not until we find Mom," Dad said. "Talking to him might lead to something, a nugget of information we can use. Xander, I'll try anything." He looked directly into Xander's eyes. *"Anything."*

Xander lowered his eyes to stare at a button on Dad's shirt. He said, "I should just go home. *You* deal with him."

Dad leaned closer. He whispered, "I need you, son. Help me figure this guy out. Maybe you'll catch something I miss."

Xander ground his teeth together. He said, "You can't trust him. It's a trick or a trap."

"So we go into it with our eyes open," Dad said. "Right?"

"Yeah," Xander said. "But if he tries anything . . ."

"Then we'll put him in his place. Together."

Xander still didn't like it. Would Abraham Van Helsing have gone out for *pie* with Dracula? No way. Just a quick stake through the heart, get it done. Then again, if Dracula had Van Helsing's mom . . .

"Yeah," Xander agreed. "Let's see what he wants."

CHAPTER

THURSDAY, 7:37 P.M.

Their booth was in the back, where the neighboring tables were empty. The waitress who seated them kept looking back at Taksidian, as though she sensed something not right about him. The kind of guy you hated to turn your back on.

They took their seats—Dad and Xander on one side, their adversary on the other—and Taksidian waved away the menu the waitress offered. "Slice of pecan, please," he said.

"What?" Xander said. "No children baked in a pie here?" Dad poked his leg under the table. Without taking his eyes off Taksidian, Xander said, "Nothing for me."

Noticing Dad's forehead, the waitress's face flashed a grimace of horror. He ordered coffee. When she was gone, he said, "What's this about?"

Taksidian began tapping his fingernails on the table. *Tick-tick-tick . . . tick-tick-tick.* Flesh-colored Band-Aids covered the bases of two fingers. Blood had seeped through. A thread-thin rivulet ran from under one of them and over three knuckles. His eyes, the olive color of army fatigues, turned from Xander to Dad. He said, "Let's deal."

Xander leaned forward, pressing his stomach against the table. He said, "How about this? You stop trying to hurt us and give my mother back. Now."

*Tick-tick-tick.* "Okay," Taksidian said.

Xander shifted uncomfortably on the bench. He glanced at Dad, who seemed to be doing nothing more than studying the other man's features—the way Roy Scheider had eyed the shark before blowing its head off in *Jaws*. He cleared his throat. "Okay?"

"Okay," Taksidian repeated.

Dad said, "What do you want in return?"

"The house. Free and clear. And you gone."

Dad shook his head. "It's not that simple—"

Taksidian raised his hand, stopping him. "It is that simple,

Ed. I know the property is held by an irrevocable trust, which means it cannot be sold, and the only people who may legally live in it are those in the King bloodline. However, I am a man of many resources. My attorneys assure me they can break the trust—with your consent, of course." The long fingers of the hand not ticking against the table pushed the hair up off his forehead and smoothed the tangle of curls that covered his scalp.

*Tick-tick-tick . . . tick-tick-tick.*

Taksidian smiled. "Yes or no?"

"How do we know you have my wife?" Dad said.

Xander thought Taksidian's smooth demeanor cracked a little. He wasn't sure what made him think so: a twitch of his mouth or a blink that wasn't calculated and timed. Taksidian said, "I thought that was a foregone conclusion."

It was Dad's turn to lean forward. He said, "*Nothing* about that house is conclusive."

Taksidian glared at him. The ticking stopped.

The waitress returned. As she lowered the plate with Taksidian's pie, he pushed it away and said, "To go, sweetie."

She pulled it back as though he had slapped her hand. She set down a cup, saucer, and coffee decanter, and stormed off, her shoes loudly spanking the floor.

Taksidian broke eye contact with Dad to glance absently around the room. "Well," he said. "You think about it. In the meantime, let me extend a hand of good faith." He gripped

Xander with his freaky, intense stare. "The two of you destroyed my house, young man."

"You attacked me!" Xander snapped.

The man's gaze flicked to Dad, back to Xander. "You misunderstood my intentions. Regardless . . ." *Tick-tick-tick* . . .

Again with the ticking. It was driving Xander nuts.

Taksidian continued: "You also demolished a vehicle, a car I believe does not belong to you. It's owned by a Dan Rainey, correct?"

Xander looked at Dad. The car, the house . . . it was all a mess that would bring in the cops. How were they going to explain it without their whole bag of secrets spilling open? Was this just the trouble the police were looking for to arrest Dad—not on some trumped-up charges paid for by Taksidian, but for real and for good this time? Then Child Services would step in and take him, Dae, and Toria away, leaving the house for Taksidian to do with as he wanted.

Dad must have been thinking the same things. He was trying to play it cool, but Xander knew his father. The concern was in his eyes, in a few beads of sweat that had broken out at his hairline.

When Taksidian spoke, his voice was softer, affecting a graciousness Xander knew the man was incapable of feeling. "To demonstrate my sincerity about wanting to resolve our differences," he said, "I'm willing to overlook this afternoon's incident. What's a little bricks and mortar among—"

He stopped. Xander knew he had been about to say, *among friends*, but realized that using that word would have sent Xander over the edge.

Instead, Taksidian moved on: "I'll even make everything right with Mr. Rainey. He doesn't have to know what happened to the car he lent you, only that he got a new one out of the deal."

"Why would you do that?" Dad asked.

The waitress dropped a bag on the table and moved off.

"Let's just say," Taksidian said, "that I'm not the bad guy you've made me out to be."

*Yeah, right*, Xander thought. He made fists under the table. His father wrapped his hand around one of them, gave it a squeeze. Xander said, "You think buying Dan a car makes up for taking my mother, for . . . for . . ." He was so furious, he couldn't finish.

"Not at all," Taksidian said. "But it is a gesture. While you consider my proposal." He slid out of the booth, adjusted his overcoat, and picked up the bag. "But don't think about it too long. There are already . . . *activities* set in motion that could spoil our negotiations. It will take some doing to stop these events, and I'll need to start right away."

"What activities?" Dad said sharply. He had abandoned his attempt to remain cool.

This was Taksidian's first threat since they'd started talking, and it didn't sit well with him. Xander thought if his son weren't in his way, Dad would have sprung up and grabbed the man.

Taksidian shrugged. "Same ol' stuff," he said. "You know."

Through gritted teeth, Dad said, "If you come near my family or my house again . . ."

Taksidian raised his brows as if to say, *What? What can you do?*

Dad answered the look: "I'll forget about repercussions. I'll make sure you *can't* hurt us ever again, you understand?"

"Ed, Ed," Taksidian said, as if to a slow child. "Let's not go there. Not after we've come so far. I'll take care of my house and Mr. Rainey's car. You think about my proposal." With that, he stepped away. He stopped and turned back, absently rubbing his injured fingers. He said, "Bring something home for your other boy. I think he's hungry."

CHAPTER

#

THURSDAY, 7:46 P.M.

Xander watched Taksidian toss cash on the counter by the register and push through the door, causing a little bell above it to jingle. Through the window, he saw the man climb into his car and drive away.

He turned to Dad. "Give him the house. Who cares? If we can get Mom—"

"We can't," Dad said. "Not through him. He doesn't have

77

her. If he did, he would have offered something that proved he could fulfill his end of the bargain."

"But . . ." Xander's thoughts were slamming around inside his skull. "Didn't he have her taken in the first place?"

"Probably." Dad pulled the cup and saucer closer, poured in some coffee. "But I think it was to scare us away. It worked with my dad. It's a lot cleaner to scare a family off in such a way that they're afraid of ever coming back."

"And," Xander said, realizing the evil beauty—if there ever could be such a thing—of Taksidian's scheme, "if a family believes their battle is with the supernatural, not some human kidnapper, what are they going to do? Risk going to the loony bin or having the house taken away to be examined by the government for a thousand years? Either way, they've lost. They'll never see their loved one again."

Dad nodded. "I think Taksidian either *lost* Mom or he never had access to her once Phemus took her away. But now he realizes we don't scare as easily as *my* father did, and he's bluffing about returning her. Maybe he thinks we'll fall for it and then realize we've been had only after it's too late, after he has legal possession of the house. Then he'd really be able to kick us out."

Xander's heart felt like someone had played baseball with it. He said, "Then why take care of the house and Dan's car? Wouldn't they cause us enough trouble to get the cops on his side?"

"As I said before, he's not doing that for us," Dad said. "He's cleaning up the evidence against himself. The body parts, the sculpture."

"If all he has to do is clean it up, he can do that overnight," Xander said. "Seems a small thing compared to finally getting rid of us."

Dad shook his head. "Crime scene investigations are pretty sophisticated these days. With trace evidence—microscopic bits of DNA that seeped into the floorboards or something—he'd have to replace that whole room, which is probably what he's planning to do. But that'll take time. He doesn't want the cops looking into the destruction of your friend's car. That would lead them right back to his house—"

"And he doesn't want them snooping around there," Xander finished, nodding. He stared down at the fake wood grain of the Formica tabletop. He drummed his fingers, realized that was what Taksidian had done, and stopped. Quietly, he said, "Then there's that other thing."

"What?"

"The future," Xander said, throwing a glance at Dad. "Even if we could give up the house for Mom . . . would we?"

Jesse had said saving the world from the awful future he had shown them was the reason they'd come to the house. Xander didn't buy it, but if they *could* fix the future, it meant figuring out what Taksidian had done and using the portals to undo it.

Dad frowned.

Xander pressed him: "If it came down to saving Mom or the future, which would you chose?"

"I don't have to decide, Xander. We can do both."

Xander picked at a gouge in the table. He hoped Dad was right.

CHAPTER

# Seventeen

THURSDAY, 8:45 P.M.

Dad and Xander stepped into the foyer of their house and slammed the door.

"Lucy, I'm home!" Xander called. He had never seen a single episode of *I Love Lucy*, but he knew the line. His nerves had calmed on the walk from town; now he was just glad to be home.

David appeared at the top of the staircase. He was wearing

*Avatar: The Last Airbender* pajama bottoms and a white T-shirt. The clothes, coupled with a big grin that broke out on his face when he saw them, gave him the appearance of a boy even younger than twelve.

"Hey," Dad said. "Where is everybody?" He sounded a lot more anxious than Xander felt.

"Keal's up here, working on the walls Phemus knocked down," David said, hurrying down. "I'm helping . . . now. I needed a shower first. Toria's in her room."

David's bare feet hit the foyer floor, and to Xander's surprise, he didn't run to Dad, but to him. David threw his arms around Xander. "I thought Taksidian got you," he said. "Until I talked to Dad and he said you were all right. I was so scared."

"Me too—for you." He really had been. Xander had even prayed that David had gotten away. And when they couldn't find him, when they'd called into the woods and he hadn't answered, Xander's stomach had twisted like an old rag.

David stepped back and brushed his hair away from his eyes. He glanced at Dad, and his mouth dropped open. "What happened?" He reached for Dad's forehead, but stopped short.

Dad touched the wound, which was a thin, arching scab framed by a yellow-blue-red bruise. He made a face, touched it again, more gently. "I had an unfriendly encounter with a steering wheel," he said. He used his fingers to comb his hair over his forehead.

David turned to Xander. "Did you see Taksidian?"

"Oh, yeah," Xander said. "You're not going to believe—"

"Excuse me . . . pardon me . . ." Dad said, grabbing David, lifting him and giving him a fierce bear hug.

"Uhhh," David moaned. "I can't breathe."

Dad set him down, mussed David's hair, and said, "Sounds like you had an adventure too."

David's eyes got wide. "I found another portal—to Taksidian's house! Want to see?"

"David was sealed up in a little room," Toria said from the top of the stairs.

Keal appeared behind her, tape measure in hand, plaster dust coating his face and clothes. Both of them started down.

"Keal knocked a big hole in the wall with a sledgehammer! He looked like—who's that guy you said?"

"John Henry," Keal laughed. "The mighty steel-driving man."

Dad met Keal at the bottom of the stairs and shook his hand. "Keal," he said, "thank you."

"Well," Keal said, "seemed like you had your hands full at the time."

"We have a lot to talk about," Dad said. "All of us."

"Let's do it in the kitchen," Xander said. "I'm starving."

"You're *not* starving," David informed him. "You're just hungry."

Xander gave him a puzzled look. "Uh . . . okay."

"You don't want to eat your foot, do you?" David asked him.

"Not today," Xander said. "What—?"

"Nobody has to eat any feet," Keal said, brushing past them to get to the kitchen. "Toria made mac 'n' cheese."

"With little bits of hot dog," David said approvingly.

"Dae ate like a pig," Toria reported. "I had to make another batch."

David simply smiled.

Toria stepped between Dad and Xander and took each of them by the hand. "I saved you some."

CHAPTER

# eighteen

Thursday, 9:05 p.m.

David sat on the kitchen counter, Toria on his right, the sink on his left. He watched Dad and Xander finish their bowls of food. They were leaning back against the island, near enough for David to kick them if he had wanted to. The kitchen was big, but they had positioned themselves in a tight group, as if instinctively knowing they needed to be close.

Only Keal stood away, his rump wedged into the elbow of

the L-shaped counter, near the pantry. But he could have been right among them, one of the family, David thought. He knew the others felt the same.

The way Keal's big arms crossed over his chest, he looked like the military officer he once was, assessing his troops. And that made David realize the man wasn't *family* as much as he was a *comrade-in-arms*: almost as close as family, but a lot more useful in the heat of battle.

David told Dad and Xander about going through Taksidian's pantry to the bone-filled chamber—and totally freaking out. Toria and Keal described hearing, then finding, then rescuing David.

"Then I fell backward into the chamber," David said, "and went back to Taksidian's pantry!"

"Dae *bit* him," Toria said, excited. "There was *blood* in his mouth!"

"Taksidian's?" Xander said. He made a disgusted face, looked into his bowl, then set it on the counter.

"What would *you* have done?" David said.

"Exactly what you did," Dad answered, "if my mind were as quick as yours. Good job."

"Hey," Keal said, "if the choice is between making a meal of Taksidian or letting him get his hands on you, *bon appétit*, David."

"Dad," Xander said, suddenly smiling. "That's what Taksidian meant at the diner."

Dad grinned at David. "He said we should get takeout for you. He thought you were hungry."

Keal laughed out loud, and that got the rest of them going.

"His fingers were all bandaged up and bleeding," Xander said. "Way to go, Dae."

"It wasn't funny at the time," he said. But the praise felt like a warm blanket on a cold day.

"Or afterward," Toria said. "He almost puked."

"It tasted gross," David said, wiping his mouth as though something of it remained.

"That's not the half of it," Keal told Dad. "Taksidian followed David back into the chamber."

"He was right there," Toria said, "grabbing at Dae!" Her hands shot out to show them, and she almost fell off the counter. David swung his broken arm around, catching her.

"What happened?" Xander's eyes were cartoon-wide.

Keal shrugged. "Chased him away."

"With the sledgehammer!" Toria added.

Dad said, "But he can come through . . . anytime?"

"I got it boarded up," Keal said. "No one's getting into the house that way."

"Well, I know one thing," Xander said. "The Brady Bunch never had a dinnertime conversation like *this*." He told the others about his face-off with Taksidian, the sculpture of body parts, Dad plowing Xander's classmate's car into Taksidian's house, the conversation with their pecan pie–eating nemesis.

David realized his mouth was hanging open. He looked around to see Toria and Keal staring at Xander with the same stunned expression.

"This guy, Taksidian," Keal said finally, "he's all over us, like dirt on a pig." He shook his head. "He even bugged the phones."

Dad had collected them—even the cordless home phone—wrapped them in a towel, and put them in a box in the sunroom, where they hardly ever went.

"It's not really bugging," Xander said. "I saw it in a movie last year. It's called an infinity transmitter. It lets someone dial any number and listen through the mouthpiece. The phone doesn't ring. It just opens a connection."

"Sounds like bugging to me," David said.

Xander shrugged. "Except there's no bug."

"We have too much going on not to have phones," Keal said. "We *need* communication."

Dad set his bowl down, thinking. "We'll pick up some pre-paid mobile phones with new numbers tomorrow. He could have got our old numbers anywhere. Mine's on our checks. Xander's is on his school records." He crossed his arms. "What I want to know is, how are we going to keep this place safe?"

"I'll have the walls back up tomorrow," Keal said. "Extra fortified."

"I don't think the walls matter," David said. "Sorry, but I

was there when Phemus knocked them down. I don't think he broke a sweat."

"We have to make something that'll *scare* him away," Xander said, "like Jesse said. Young Jesse."

On one of their trips through a portal, the boys had found themselves in 1931, where they'd met Jesse at age fourteen. He had told him how to keep time travelers out of the house.

"You mean the wall lights?" Keal asked.

"They're carved to resemble whatever superstition scares the people you're trying to keep out. As long as they have a strong enough fear of something, it works," Xander explained.

Dad said, "Maybe something about going through time makes them especially susceptible to being scared. I jump at my own shadow when I go over."

"One problem," David said. "What scares Phemus?"

The guy was huge, maybe seven feet tall and muscular. It was hard to imagine anything frightening him.

"We have to know where he comes from," Dad said. "What civilization, what era." He pointed. "Toss me that, will you, honey?"

Toria looked beside her at several lunch-size bags of chips. She whipped one his way.

"Me too," David said.

Toria shook her head and handed him one.

Dad popped a chip into his mouth and said, "So, what do we know about Phemus?"

"He's ugly," Toria said.

"He wears animal pelts," David mumbled through a mouthful of Fritos.

Xander lifted himself to sit on the island. He said, "He has lots of scars."

Dad nodded. "If only . . ." His eyes grew big. "Wait here." He darted around the island and disappeared out the kitchen door. His feet pounded up the stairs.

Toria looked around the room. Xander shrugged.

Keal grinned and said, "Toria . . . sweetheart . . . ?"

She hurled a chip bag across the kitchen to him.

Still chowing, David said, "So where do you find big, ugly, pelt-wearing guys who get hurt a lot?"

"Professional wrestling," Xander said.

Dad clopped back down the stairs. When he entered, he was holding one hand behind his back. He said, "What's the best way to know where a guy comes from?"

"Ask him," David said.

"A birth certificate," Keal said.

Dad rolled his eyes. "Besides that."

They all looked blank.

"Language," Dad said. He pulled Toria's toy bear, Wuzzy, from behind his back and plopped it on the island.

# nineteen

THURSDAY, 9:18 P.M.

On the night Phemus took Mom, he'd spoken to Toria. Her teddy bear, which contained a built-in recorder, had saved his words.

Now Dad adjusted Wuzzy on the counter. He said, "Every race, every civilization, every nationality possesses its own unique language or a unique dialect of a more common language. I've heard that some linguists can tell where a person grew up just by how he speaks."

"Professor Higgins!" Toria said. "*My Fair Lady*. You know it, Xander."

"Hey," Xander said defensively. "You're the one who likes musicals."

"Henry Higgins said he could tell where someone is from just by hearing them talk."

"And be accurate within six miles," Dad agreed. "That's real. Some guys are even better, and their scope of known languages and dialects covers the whole world."

"Yeah," Xander said, "but does it cover all of history too?"

Dad pointed at him. "Some people specialize in ancient languages. It's called philology."

Keal looked into his chip bag and shook it. "You know any philologists?"

"As a matter of fact, I do," Dad said. "An old college buddy of mine. He teaches at UCLA." He patted Wuzzy on the head and rushed out of the room. He turned into the library, where most of his office things were still in boxes, and called out, "I have his number here somewhere."

Toria crinkled her brow. "Wuzzy's going to help us find out what scares Phemus?"

"That's what Dad thinks," Xander said, sounding skeptical.

Toria smiled over at Wuzzy, like a proud parent.

Dad hurried in, flipping through the pages of a small

notebook. "Here it is," he said. "Mike Patterson. Where's the phone?" He froze and grimaced, remembering.

Keal crumpled his chip bag and tossed it into the trash can. He crossed his arms. "We don't want Taksidian knowing we're figuring this out," he said. "He'll try to stop us for sure."

Dad frowned at the notebook. "Does that infinite thing—"

"Infinity transmitter," Xander said.

"Does it work if you're on the phone, or just when the phone's not in use?" Dad asked. "Can he listen in on telephone conversations? If it just opens up the mike, I wouldn't think so."

Xander shrugged. "I don't know." He looked up at the ceiling, thinking. "In the movie, they used it to hear people who weren't talking *on* the phone, only near it."

"I think it's a risk we have to take," Dad said. "Who knows when Phemus will attack again? The sooner we scare him away, the better."

"We know he has the mobile phone numbers," Keal said. "Use the land line, just in case."

"Has he ever called here?" Dad asked.

"He never called our mobile phones either," Xander said, "but he must have known the numbers."

"I'm going to do it," Dad said. He walked out of the kitchen through the butler's pantry, which led to the sunroom.

"He's excited," Toria observed.

Xander sighed loudly. " 'Bout time."

"Hey," David said, tired of Xander's grousing about Dad's lack of action. "He tailed Taksidian with us. He drove a car into a brick wall to save you." David threw up his hands. "And he saved your butt before, too, from that gladiator. Dad does stuff."

Xander put on his guilty face. "You're right," he said. "Sorry."

"Say we figure out what scares Phemus," Keal said. "What next? We carve a wall light?"

Xander nodded. "That's what Jesse said. I think he made most of the ones upstairs."

"Who knows how to carve?" Keal said.

"I can whittle," David said.

"Okay," Keal said. "I crown you Chief Wall Light Maker."

Dad dashed into the kitchen, the clunky home phone pressed against his cheek. He said, "I appreciate this, Mike. Hold on, here it is." He punched the speaker button and set the phone beside Wuzzy. He looked up at the others and touched his finger to his lips: *Shhhh*. He flipped a switch on Wuzzy's back and squeezed the bear's paw to start the playback.

Toria's voice came out of the bear: "Good night, Xander. Thanks for watching over me."

"Oops," Dad said, reaching for the paw. "Wrong memory chip. Hold on, Mike."

Before he could change the recording, Wuzzy said with

David's voice, "I am too," and Toria replied, "Thank you, David."

David felt a hollowness in his chest, as though his heart had deflated a little. He remembered that conversation. He and Xander had volunteered to sleep with Toria because she said a big man had been in her room. A nightmare, they had thought at the time. Mom was home, and all was right with the world. Mom tucked them in and said good night. And the next time they saw her, Phemus was carrying her away.

Dad squeezed the paw a few times.

Wuzzy played Toria saying, "Who is it?" in a sleepy voice.

"Okay, Mike," Dad said. "It's coming up."

Creaking noises came out of Wuzzy, then:

Toria: "Who—"

A deep, rumbling voice: *"Sas ehei na erthete na paiksei."*

David felt sick.

Dad grabbed the paw and waited. After a few moments, he said, "Well? Mike?"

Silence.

"Mike?"

"Uh," came a staticky voice from the phone's puny speaker. "I recognize some diphthong patterns, but . . . could you play it again? Turn the phone speaker off and hold the handset up to the recorder."

Dad did, then brought the phone up to his face. He let out a heavy breath. "I see. I understand." Then he brightened.

"You can? You'll do that? When?" He darted out of the room, heading for the library.

David looked at his sister, then his brother. Their faces were as glum as he knew his was. He said, "Hard to hear that voice."

Xander nodded.

Toria sniffed, wiped a tear off her cheek.

David hopped down from the counter and went to her. "We'll get Mom back," he told her. "That's what we're doing now, working on it, you know." He was speaking to himself as much as to her.

She tried to smile. She sniffed again. A tear streaked down, and David smeared it away. Xander walked over with a paper towel.

Dad appeared in the doorway. He glanced at them all, then his eyes stopped on Toria. "Are you okay?"

"I'm all right," she said.

He went to her and ran his hand over her head, down the length of her hair. "This will work out," he said. "I promise." His eyes found David's, then Xander's.

"What'd your friend say?" Xander asked.

"Inflections and subtle tones are crucial in his work. The phone line was flattening out the words too much. He thinks if he could hear Wuzzy live and in person, he could tell us something."

"So, what?" Xander said. "We send Wuzzy to him?"

"Well . . ." Dad said, a sly smile creasing his mouth. "Wuzzy's too valuable to entrust to the postal service, and as I said, the sooner the better. So Toria and I are *taking* Wuzzy to see Mike. We leave tomorrow."

CHAPTER

THURSDAY, 10:43 P.M.

David lay in his bed, arms crossed under his head. He watched the moonlight reflected on his ceiling and the way the shadows from tree branches danced through it in the wind.

"Xander?" he said.

"Hmmm?" his brother answered from his bed.

"I've been thinking," David said. "Something weird happened today."

"No kidding!"

"I mean, something *else*. In the Civil War, when I went into the hospital tent looking for Dr. Scott . . . I think I saw Nana."

"You think?" Xander rolled onto his side, propping his head up.

"She was facing away from me, feeding some wounded guy." David relived the moment in his mind and felt the chilly-footed insect scamper along his spine again. "But her hair . . . something about her . . . I'm almost positive it was her. But how could that be? We rescued her yesterday."

"I guess when we go back to the same place we've been before, we can go back *earlier* than the previous time."

David scrunched his brows together, thinking. "That's too weird," he said.

"Don't think about it too hard," Xander said, falling back onto his pillow. "Your brain will explode."

They were silent for a few minutes, David trying to get his mind off the so-freaky-your-brain-will-explode aspects of time travel. Finally, he said, "What do you think of Dad taking Wuzzy to that philanthropy guy?"

"Philology," Xander corrected.

"Sounds like somebody who studies people named Phil."

"Maybe there are Davidologists too," Xander said. "That'd sure take an advanced degree, figuring *you* out."

On the ceiling, two leafy branches looked like tall, skinny

guys with shields and swords. They were bending in toward each other, thrusting and parrying and generally trying to slaughter one another. Then they'd back off, shaking and twitching, as if each was taunting the other.

*I've definitely gone through too many portals,* David thought. *I'm seeing battles everywhere.*

In almost every world, there had been some kind of war or fighting or mortal danger. Not for the first time, he wondered why that was. *Young Jesse's world,* he thought. *No fighting there . . . for some reason.* He suspected a pattern guided all of it, none of it was random, but for the life of him he couldn't figure it out. The thought struck him that it might actually *be* the life of him if he didn't figure it out.

"So," he said, "what do you think? Dad taking off?"

"Good idea," Xander said. He was silent awhile, then said, "*If* that guy can figure out Phemus's language. I have my doubts."

David rolled onto his side and folded the pillow under his head. "You think we can keep Phemus out—with just a *lamp?*"

Xander ran a hand over his face and groaned. "I don't know, Dae. Stranger things have happened in this house. Besides, symbols and things like that scare people. They always have. Vampires hate crosses."

"Vampires aren't real," David said.

"Okay," Xander said. He turned on his side to face his brother. "The Vikings carved dragon heads onto the prows of their ships. Historians say they scared the tar out of people."

"That's because of the Vikings," David said. "Not the dragon's head. We should know that better than anyone." Only that morning, he and Xander had barely survived an attack of Viking Berserkers.

"Of course it's what the symbol *stands for*, not the symbol itself," Xander said. "Say you're a villager in eleventh-century England. You've seen Viking raiders ransack villages and slaughter innocent people."

David nodded.

"You're out traveling," Xander continued, "and come up to the big wooden gates of a town. But there's a huge symbol painted on them: a Viking dragon. What do you do?"

"Run away like my butt's on fire," David said.

"Exactly," Xander said. "You were scared by a symbol. The symbol *becomes* what's behind it."

"At least we're more sophisticated now," David said.

"Don't be so sure. Think about it. Remember the first portal you went through, to that jungle with the tigers?"

"And warriors," David added. His stomach lurched the way it had when he was on the shaky rope bridge over a deep gorge. Warriors on one side, tigers on the other. He shivered and closed his eyes.

"What if," Xander said, "the first thing you saw when you went over was a skull-and-crossbones? You know, the symbol for danger. It was slathered on a tree in what looked like blood. Real bones piled under it—or a whole skeleton!"

"Yeah," David said, getting it. "I would have turned around and dived right back through the portal before it disappeared. Straight back to the antechamber." The idea that wall lights could actually scare people away suddenly made more sense.

Silence filled the room. The house creaked around them. *Just the house creaking*, David thought. He turned onto his stomach and lay there watching his brother roll one way and then the other. His eyelids grew heavy, and he let them close.

"Dae?" Xander said softly.

"Hmmm?"

"I was thinking," Xander said. "What if Taksidian's not human?"

David's eyes snapped open. "What?"

"What if he's like . . . I don't know, a demon?"

"Knock it off," David said.

"I mean, he's *mean* enough. He's creepy looking. He's got that statue made out of body parts."

David raised his head. "Are you *trying* to scare me?"

"I'm just saying."

"Well, stop saying," David said. He flopped his face into his pillow. He waited for Xander to speak again, then he was dreaming: he was running down the third-floor hallway, chased by Taksidian . . . only the hallway never ended, and Taksidian's face was a ghoulish demon's.

# twenty-one

FRIDAY, 5:18 A.M.

After the nightmare, David had no dreams at all. Just sleep. Rest. Respite from the craziness of his life, from using muscles and joints that were battered and sore. Peace.

Too soon: a nudge, someone shaking his shoulder.

"David?" The voice was deep, rumbly. "I'm going back to see Jesse. Want to come?"

"Keal?" David asked. Déjà vu, he thought. Déjà vu in a dream. How weird.

"Hey," Keal said. More nudges. "Want to see Jesse?"

In his half-awake state, David heard the words, but didn't make all the connections. "Jesse?" he said. "Back at the house?"

"At the hospital," Keal said. He shook David. "Wake up if you want to go."

"Young Jesse?"

"Old Jesse!" Xander said from his bed. He propped himself up on his elbow and addressed Keal. "Dae's still dreaming. I want to go."

"Get your clothes on," Keal said.

"Wait," David said. He threw back his blankets. Groaning, he sat up and hooked his legs over the side of the bed. "I want to see Jesse too." He rubbed his face, scratched the top of his head. "Oh, man, was I out."

"You know we're talking about Old Jesse, right?" Xander said, rolling out of bed.

"Old Jesse, yeah." David stood, steadying himself on Keal's shoulder, then stumbled toward the dresser. "I like Old Jesse," he said, trying to wake himself up by talking, having to think. "I like Young Jesse too. He's probably a kid I would hang out with, if I, you know, lived back then. I think I'd like Jesse at any age."

"Maybe you'll get a chance to find out," Xander said, tugging on his jeans. "Maybe we'll meet thirty-year-old Jesse and middle-aged Jesse."

Keal stood and walked to the door. "This conversation is

just too weird for me, boys," he said. "I'll see you downstairs. If you hurry, you can see your father and Toria before they head to the airport."

••••••••

David had showered the evening before, after escaping from the chamber. Even so, he took another one now. He figured he'd stumble through the day half asleep if he didn't. It was like some exhaustion fairy was keeping track of his lack of sleep, stress, and physical exertion. *Ran from Berserkers? Let's put this rock right here on your head. Didn't get a full eight hours' sleep? Rocks for both shoulders. Worried about Mom? Two rocks here and three rocks there . . .*

He was surprised how many of those rocks fell away under the cold spray of the shower. Even more when he lathered up with a bar of perky-smelling soap. By the time he cranked the water off and stepped out, he was feeling pretty close to normal. He wondered how big the pile of stones would be by the end of the day, and what terrible thing he'd have to endure for each one.

*That's no way to think*, he told himself. *It's going to be a great day!*

He stared at the face in the mirror and said out loud, "Yeah, sure it will."

When he went downstairs, everyone was around the dining table, bowls of cereal before them.

"Hey, Dae," Dad said. "Froot Loops or Shredded Wheat?"

David plopped down in a chair beside Xander. "Is that your way of asking how I feel?" He grabbed a box at random and dumped its contents into a bowl. Turned out to be Life, which he liked. He wished his luck at choosing portals was as good.

"We should be out of the hospital by seven, plenty of time to get them to school," Keal told Dad, apparently continuing a discussion that had started before David arrived.

Dad checked his watch and looked surprised. He scooped a spoonful of colorful cereal into his mouth, pushed his chair back, and stood. He said, "Toria, we gotta go. Our flight leaves at seven thirty, and it takes almost an hour to get to Redding. Xander and David, Keal's in charge."

Munching, Keal gave Dad a thumbs-up.

Dad picked up his bowl. "Keal," he said, "would you mind swinging by to see my mom?"

"No prob—" Keal started, before the milky pieces of Honeycomb began spilling out of his mouth. He caught one in his spoon.

"Just let her know why the phones aren't working, fill her in on what's going on," Dad said. "Tell her I'll stop by tonight with Toria." He went around the table toward the kitchen, then stopped. "Oh . . . and watch for tails, maybe drive around a bit first."

Keal gave him another thumbs-up.

Dad nodded at David and Xander. "See you this evening, guys."

They said their good-byes and went back to their breakfasts.

Toria lifted her bowl to her lips and slurped down the remaining milk. She smiled at her brothers, milk mustache becoming a goatee. "Have fun at school, boys," she said, standing and turning away.

"Have fun getting frisked," Xander said.

She turned around. "What?"

"Oh, I forgot you haven't flown in a while," Xander said. "Things have changed. They frisk everyone now. It can get a little rough."

"They do *not!*"

Xander pretended to be ashamed for startling her. He said, "You're right, they probably won't be too rough on you, being a little kid and all."

Frowning, she turned and went into the kitchen.

"That was mean," David whispered.

Keal snapped a spoon of milk at Xander. It splattered over his face. David laughed.

"Hey!" Xander said, rubbing milk out of his eye. He snatched his own spoon from the bowl, but Keal was already jogging out of the room, an evil laugh rumbling out of him.

# twenty-two

FRIDAY, 6:31 A.M.

Following Keal's "Why mess with success?" strategy, they got into the hospital the same way they had the day before: Keal went in first, then opened a side door for David and Xander. The boys waited in the mustard-colored stairwell, listening to water rush through the exposed pipes, while Keal reconned the second floor.

"Think Jesse will be able to talk?" Xander asked when the

brothers were alone. He shifted from foot to foot, looking nervous.

"He did yesterday," David said. "A little."

A few minutes later, Keal cracked open the door. "We're on," he said.

Jesse hadn't moved. The right side of his bed was still cluttered with machines, monitors, and wires. The same chrome tree held what were probably different, but similar looking, bags of liquid, each trailing a tube that ran into his arm. And there was that see-through cylinder, inside which a bellows expanded and contracted in time with Jesse's lungs.

Jesse appeared pretty much the same, as well: a wisp of a man barely making a bulge in the blankets. His arms, resting at his sides, almost vanished against the bright white sheets. Blue veins mottled his cheeks, forehead, and balding scalp. Silver hair fanned out around his head like a halo.

The three of them stood at the foot of the bed, taking it all in. Keal lifted a clipboard off a hook at the foot of the bed and started reading it.

Xander made a slight moaning sound. David followed his gaze; he had spotted Jesse's hand, the stub of his missing finger bandaged over. Xander's gaze shifted to the bellows, then up to the machine that beeped along with Jesse's heart. His skin had paled to a shade only slightly less white than Jesse's.

David had planned on letting Xander talk to Jesse first, but clearly his brother wasn't ready. David slipped in front of him and approached Jesse on the uncluttered side of the bed. The old man's skin reminded him of tracing paper, thin and brittle. He touched the bandaged hand, then slipped his fingers around it—down low, near Jesse's thumb. The last thing he wanted to do was cause him pain.

He moved his attention to the thin blanket covering Jesse's chest. He saw no movement there, no rise and fall. A spark of panic shot from his brain to his heart. The monitor was beeping, beeping; the bellows gasped—but maybe they were wrong. Could they be wrong?

Then he saw it: the slightest movement over Jesse's stomach. He felt himself relax. He closed his eyes.

*You're an old woman,* he told himself. *Take it easy. Be tough for Jesse.*

He took in Jesse's face. The same twin tubes went into his nostrils, almost lost in his mustache. Silver stubble roamed the creases of his cheeks and chin like fake snow on a model railroad. His eyelids vibrated as the eyes under them moved back and forth.

"He's dreaming," David said, smiling at Keal and Xander.

"No, he's not," whispered Xander.

When David looked back, Jesse's eyes were open. His blue irises were turned toward him. They were vivid and alive, his eyes. Sparkling. So similar to Young Jesse's, it was as though they were immune to time and age and all the things they had witnessed, both awful and awesome. Jesse's mustache trembled, and he managed a thin smile.

"Hi," David said. "How do you feel?"

Jesse nodded. "Better."

"Keal and Xander are here with me."

Jesse shifted his gaze to them. His mouth parted, and he sighed. A whitish-pink tongue poked out and slid over his lips. He said, "Glad you . . . could make it."

"We saw you," David said. "We found the antechamber you wanted us to find, the one that led back to the house being built. You were there."

Jesse smiled and nodded. He said, "Just a kid."

"Yeah," David said. "You were fourteen, but I recognized you. Haven't changed that much."

Jesse tried to laugh, but wound up coughing, a thin, airy hack.

"You knew we'd meet someday," David said. The notion that Jesse had spent a lifetime with David's and Xander's faces in his memory, decades before they were born, fascinated him. This world was so much more magical and incredible than he'd ever known—than most people ever imagined. He said, "You knew when you left the house that you'd come back to help us. We told you, the young you, that you would."

Jesse's head moved on the pillow: *yes*. "Your visits," he said slowly. "They were some of the best times I ever had. Thank you."

"Visits?" Xander said.

"We go back again?" David said. "We see you again? We said we would, but I didn't really know . . ."

111

Jesse frowned. The wrinkles around his eyes came down with the corners of his mouth. "You've been there . . . only once? Once so far?"

"That was yesterday," David explained. "We haven't had time—"

Jesse shook his head *no*. "You have to get back there. Soon. So much you need to know." He strained to lift his head.

"Jesse," David said. "Take it easy."

"Promise me," he said. "Promise . . . you'll go back. Soon."

"Can't you just tell us?"

Jesse's face tightened in thought. He said, "I can't. Something—Time or changes in history or old age—is keeping the details from me, but I know you must go back, I *know* it. Tell me you will."

David looked at Xander, who said, "We will."

David told Jesse, "I promise. As soon as we can."

Jesse dropped his head down. His eyes closed.

David felt Jesse's fingers curl around his own. He watched Jesse's hand tremble as he tried to put strength into the squeeze. A pinpoint of blood appeared through the gauze where his index finger used to be.

"Jesse . . ." David said, worried.

The old man was eyeing him again. He said, "I haven't dreamed a change . . . since you saved Marguerite." The little girl David saved from a German tank. When they changed the past, Jesse sensed it as a dream, a fading memory of the way things were before the change.

"We try not to mess with things when we go over," David said. In truth, it was usually all they could do to take a quick look around for Mom and get out with their lives.

Jesse closed his eyes. Just when David thought they'd stay closed, they fluttered open. "You mustn't simply . . . do nothing."

"I don't understand," David said. "What are we supposed to do?"

"Fix things," Jesse said. "That's your purpose."

David shook his head. "You said that before, but I don't understand."

Jesse breathed in deeply, then coughed out the air. He said, "We're all put on this earth for a reason. Most people spend half their lives trying to figure out what it is they're supposed to do." He breathed, two, three breaths before continuing. "How wonderful it is to find out when you're young."

"But, Jesse," Xander said, "this? The house? Going back in time?"

Jesse smiled at Xander, and David realized Jesse knew his brother as well as he did: This is not what Xander wanted to hear. He had other plans for his life. "I can't tell you the reason, Xander," Jesse said. "But our family, our bloodline, was meant to fix things in the past, things that people have messed up." He raised his head slightly, seeming to draw energy from his words. "I don't know how far back it goes, but my father thought maybe centuries . . . even longer. Forever."

"The house hasn't been around forever," Xander said.

"And the time ripples, the portals, haven't always been where they are now," Jesse said. "They drift, they move."

David nodded. The portals in other worlds drifted around. He and Xander had witnessed it. It made sense that the currents of time here, in the present, would drift around, too. Young Jesse had told them that his father thought that building the antechambers and the portal doors might somehow lock them in place—at least for a while. Seemed he was right.

Jesse continued: "Our family has always been drawn to them, no matter where they are. When we don't fix the past—" He dropped his head back onto the pillow and scanned the ceiling, as though looking for the words he wanted. "When we don't . . . bad things happen."

"Like what?" David whispered, not sure he wanted to know.

"Wars, diseases, sorrows," Jesse said. "More grief than there has to be."

"But you left," Xander said. "Over thirty years ago, you just up and left."

"I was old even then," Jesse said. "I had a stroke. Couldn't walk or use my left arm. Some of my motor skills eventually returned, but at the time, I could no longer do my job in the house. I had been going back into history for so long, Time kept pulling on me, trying to suck me back. I had to get away. But I contacted your grandfather and told him it was his turn."

"And after Nana was kidnapped," David said, "he couldn't take it and left."

"The world is darker for it, for Time not having a Gatekeeper for so long," Jesse said. "I don't know in what ways, but I know it's true." His eye shifted to David. "Who knows how many people like Marguerite he could have saved, how much pain he could have prevented?"

David glanced at Xander, who looked as baffled as David felt. "How are we supposed to know what to fix, where to look, what to do?"

"You'll know." His eyes turned away, then found David again. "The doctor."

David turned to Keal. "He wants a doctor."

"No," Jesse said. "The one you told me about . . . in the Civil War."

"Oh yeah," David said. "There was a nurse calling for a doctor. She asked us to get him."

"Did you?" Jesse asked.

"No, we had to go."

Jesse didn't say anything, just looked into David's eyes.

"We were *supposed* to get him?" David said.

"It's your purpose," Jesse said. "The reason you and the house and that event in the Civil War came together."

"But . . . we didn't do it."

Jesse smiled. "You'll get another chance."

David looked at Xander, at Keal. He felt that something big was happening, but wasn't sure what it was.

"Jesse," he said. "I don't understand. Out of all the people who died in the Civil War, why *that* guy? Why do I have to help save *him*?"

"David," Jesse said, "your job is not to help save him."

"It's not? But—"

Jesse squeezed his hand again. "Your job is to get the doctor. That's what you were asked to do."

"Aren't they the same thing?"

Jesse waggled his head. "Maybe . . . maybe not. What happens afterward is not your concern. If someone you trust asks you to do a task, you just do it. You trust they have a good reason for asking."

"But, Jesse," David said, "who's asking?"

Jesse smiled. "Who do you think? Who set it all in motion? Who made time? Who made you?"

David opened his mouth, then closed it. He looked at Xander and Keal, but their expressions reflected his own confusion. He turned back to Jesse. He whispered, "God?"

Jesse's smile widened. His eyes slowly closed.

"Jesse?" David said.

The old man began to snore.

# twenty-three

FRIDAY, 7:13 A.M.

"You heard him," Xander said. "We need to go back to Young Jesse's time right away." He was turned sideways in the front passenger seat of Keal's rented Dodge Charger. "David promised him. Right, Dae?" He looked over the seat at David.

David shrugged, not wanting to get involved. This time, he did think Xander had a point, but he liked Keal and didn't want the guy ticked at him.

"David said you guys would do it as soon as you could," Keal said, "and that's not now." He pulled off Main Street to the frontage road that led to Pinedale Middle and Senior High School.

When Xander saw how close they were, he slapped the dash and said, "No, no, no! Come on, Keal, be cool."

Keal cast Xander a sharp eye. "You think I'm *not* cool?"

Xander looked stricken. "No . . . I mean . . . yeah, you're cool, but it's not cool we have to go to school."

Keal grinned back at David, who laughed, slapped his brother on the shoulder, and said, "He so played you."

David thought Keal was way too cool to ever *worry* about being cool. Keal didn't care if Xander thought he was cool or not.

Keal said, "Xander, I promised your dad I'd get you to school."

"Call him!" Xander said. "You're going to go buy those phones he talked about, right? That could be the first call we make. The store's like a mile from here. It'd take ten minutes."

Keal checked the clock on the dash. "He's in the air, and he doesn't have the phone. Now, stop. Don't you get tired of arguing the same thing over and over?"

Xander humphed, straightened in his seat, and folded his arms across his chest. He mumbled, "Maybe it's a teenage thing."

Keal pulled into the school's drop-off lane and waited to move forward. "Got lunch money?" he asked.

When Xander ignored him, David said, "It's on an account."

Keal pulled up, and Xander hopped out.

"Thanks, Keal," David said. "See you at three." He caught up with Xander and told him, "You shouldn't treat Keal that way."

"Why not?"

"He's on our side," David said. "He's just doing what he promised Dad. He's right, you know."

"What, that we should keep up appearances, that we go to school, even though it's doing nothing to rescue—"

He stopped, and David knew why: there were too many kids around to have this conversation. About a dozen of those kids jostled against the brothers getting through the main doors. Xander turned left, heading for the high school wing. David grabbed his arm.

"I mean you arguing the same thing over and over," David said. "We know you're gung ho and Dad's more cautious. Why can't you just go along for a while? Dad's starting to get it. He's doing more. Give him some time."

Xander got a handful of David's shirt and pulled him out of the student traffic. He pushed him against a locker and leaned close. "We don't have time," he whispered harshly. "Even Jesse thinks we don't." He lowered his gaze to his fist, entwined with the shirt and pressed against David's breastbone. He frowned, released his grip, and smoothed the material over David's chest.

Then he turned, pressed his back against a locker, and slid down until he was sitting on the floor.

David did the same, saying nothing.

"Sorry, Dae," Xander said.

They pulled their legs up to keep them from being trampled.

"Remember the other day," Xander said, "when I said it felt like things were building up, that something big was going to happen and we had to prepare for it?"

David nodded. He had been taking a bath after returning from the *Titanic*. Xander had tromped in, saying things like *We'll sleep when we're dead.* It had worried David because it seemed that his brother was going crazy from stress and frustration and exhaustion. He wanted to do everything all at once: secure the house, go into as many worlds as possible, without planning, without thought—anything to get Mom, get her now! Dad and Keal had slammed on the brakes, forcing Xander to sleep. It had helped his brother's craziness—or so David had thought.

"I still feel that way," Xander said. "Even more. All that stuff with Taksidian yesterday. What Jesse said today." He rolled his head toward David. "Don't you feel it?"

David felt a lot of things. They were juggling too many

problems—needing to find Mom, trying to survive the horrors of the worlds they had to go into to find her, staying alive in *this* world, keeping the house so they could keep looking . . . not to mention all the emotions that came with everything they'd experienced.

He said, "Feel what, exactly?"

"Like . . ." Xander rocked his head back and forth, thinking. "Like there's a ticking bomb under us, and it's getting ready to go off."

David nodded. "Now that you put it that way."

"Dae," Xander said, "I don't think we have all the time in the world. I don't think Mom does."

"So what are we supposed to do?"

"I don't—" Xander stopped. He looked down the hallway, one way, then the other. The mass of kids had thinned out as they hurried to class before first bell. "Yes, I do know." He stood, then helped David up.

"What?" David said.

"What we can, when we can," he said with a smile David didn't like. "Right?"

"Well . . . yeah." Simple enough. David still had to get to his locker before class. He said, "I gotta go—"

"Listen," Xander interrupted. "Just after class starts, meet me in the bathroom."

"What? Why?"

"Just do it, okay?"

David thought about it. He shook his head. "I can't get out of class. Mrs. Moreau . . . the other day she told one kid she didn't care if his bladder burst, that he should have thought about it before class."

"Then we won't go to class," Xander said. He grabbed David's sleeve. "Come on."

David pulled his arm away. "Wait. Why?"

Xander looked around. "We're getting out of here. Can't you hear it? The house is calling us."

# CHAPTER

# twenty-four

"What do you mean, the house is calling us?" David said.

Xander didn't answer. He just grabbed David's sleeve again and pulled him toward the bathroom on the cafeteria side of the school.

David sighed and fell into step beside his brother.

They passed the middle school classrooms on the left. The right wall was mostly windows, looking out on the front court-yard and, beyond it, the drop-off and pickup lane. David craned his head around to see the west end of the courtyard, where the administration wing—and Dad's office—was. As they walked, the outbuilding that contained the auto shop came into view. It was there that Taksidian had stood yesterday, watching for them. Instead, David, Xander, and Dad had waited for him to leave so they could follow him. He wasn't there now.

They were approaching the end of the main hallway. The bathrooms were around the corner, in a shorter hall that housed lockers, but no classrooms. Then it dawned on him what Xander was planning. He said, "Xander, wait. You're not thinking about—"

"Alexander King!" The voice came from behind them, bold and sharp as broken bones.

Xander turned. He said, "Uh-oh."

A boy about seventeen years old strode toward them. He was scowling so severely, his entire brow make a ledge above his eyes. His arms swung like a marching soldier's. He wore a tight T-shirt that showed off the hours he'd spent working out. His pecs bulged, his arms strained the shirt's armholes.

"Who—?" David started.

"Dan Rainey," Xander answered.

"The car guy? But I thought Taksidian . . ."

The guy marched right up to Xander, bumping his chest into Xander's considerably less developed one. "What'd you do to my car, dawg?"

Xander had to tip his head way back to look Dan in the face. He said, "I . . . uh . . ."

David inched away from his brother. He would need the room to pivot around and bring his cast up into Dan's cranium. There was still enough plaster under the Ace bandage that it should do some damage. Enough, anyway, to give them a fair head start for the door. Yeah, it would hurt—might even rebreak his arm—but not as much as Dan's fists.

"I'll tell you what you did," Dan yelled, spraying spittle into Xander's face. "You showed it to Jimbo." His face lit up, suddenly sporting a toothy grin and happy eyes. "Dude!" He raised his palm high in the hair.

Xander, his face morphing into a comical blend of fear and puzzlement, slapped Dan's hand. He backed away a step, wiped his face.

"I *knew* my little Buggy was a sweet ride," Dan said, "but Jimbo flipped for it, man. Said he had one like it in college and had to have it."

"Jimbo?" Xander said.

"Jim . . . Jim . . ." Dan said, scrunching his face, searching for a last name. "You know . . ."

"Taksidian?" David said.

"That's it," Dan said. "How ya doing, little dude?" He backhanded David's shoulder.

David rubbed the spot. "Better," he said, and thought, *Now that you're not going to kill my brother.*

"He's one creepy dude, isn't he?" Dan said. "That Jimbo. Oops, sorry . . . what is he, your uncle or something?"

"Something," Xander said.

"Hey, listen," Dan said, becoming serious. "I know I should probably give you something. You know, a finder's fee. But me and my dad are going car shopping this weekend, and I don't know what I'm going to need. Those add-ons can get expensive, I hear. GPS, thousand-watt amps, stuff like that."

"That's okay," Xander said. "I'm just glad you're cool with the deal."

"Cool? Ha! I'm ice cold." He cocked his head, seeming to think about his words. "Ice cold in a *good* way," he clarified. "Hey, gotta run. Thanks, buddy. I owe you one." He sought another high five, and Xander gave it to him. Then he was off, marching down the long hall.

"That guy's in your class?" David asked.

"I think he was held back."

"Taksidian works fast."

"Yeah," Xander said, something on his mind. "He does."

"Now I do have to go to the bathroom," David said. He hurried around the corner, past the lockers, where some kids were still mingling, and into the bathroom.

A boy was washing his hands when they entered. David stepped up to a urinal. Xander pushed open each of the three stall doors. The kid left, and David went to the sink.

"David," Xander whispered. "Get in." He jerked his head toward a stall. "Hurry."

"Xander—"

"Hurry. There are always last-minute potty-breakers. Get in before they see us."

David shook his head and went into the stall.

"Lock the door," Xander instructed. "Put your feet up." He went into the next stall.

"You're going through the locker portal, aren't you?" David whispered.

"Shhh."

Someone entered the bathroom. A urinal flushed. Footsteps echoed away.

*Oh, wash your hands,* David thought.

"You can't go through the locker," he said. "We're supposed to be in school. They'll tell Dad."

"This is our chance, Dae," Xander said. "Do what we can, when we can, remember?"

"Yeah, but—"

"This is *when.* Old Jesse said to get back to see Young Jesse soon. It's important. Keal's not going to be home for a while. He's gotta get the phones and visit Nana."

"We can do it just as easily after school," David said. "Why *now?*"

"Tick, tick, tick," Xander said.

"That's not fair. It doesn't mean you can just—"

A urinal flushed.

David froze. He even stopped breathing.

A shadow stirred on the tiles under the stall door. Sneakered feet stepped into view. Knees touched the floor, a hand. Anthony's face peered under the door. He was one of three kids who had befriended David the first day of school.

"David!" Anthony said. "What are you doing?"

"Nothing. You always snoop on people in the toilet?"

Anthony grinned. "Only when someone's hiding. Who are you talking to?"

"My brother."

Xander said, "Go away."

"You going to skip?" Anthony said. "Your dad's the *principal*." The idea obviously amazed him.

"Don't tell anybody," David said. "Okay?"

"Tell who what?" he said and laughed.

The bell rang.

"Oh, crumb," Anthony said and vanished, leaving only his echoing footsteps.

"Now what?" David said.

"Give the hall five minutes to clear," Xander said. "Now be quiet."

An order easy for David's mouth to obey. Not so easy for his heart.

# CHAPTER

# twenty-five

FRIDAY, 7:30 A.M.

Standing in front of the motel door, Keal scanned the parking lot. Only a few parked cars, none with anyone inside as far as he could tell. He watched the street in front of the complex. A van cruised past, then a car heading the other direction. Neither had slowed or revealed people inside who appeared interested in the place. Satisfied he hadn't been followed and that the room wasn't being watched, he knocked.

The curtain behind a window pushed back, and he waved. Nana opened the door. Her hair was disheveled and her eyes were red, as though she had been crying.

"Are you all right?" he asked.

She touched her cheek, tried to smile. "I've been so worried. What's going on? How's everyone? How's *Jesse?*"

Keal gave her a big grin. "Everyone's fine," he said, stepping in. "The boys and I just saw Jesse at the hospital. He's better." He held up a cup and a plastic bag dangling from the same hand. "Coffee and bagels, courtesy of 7-11."

She pressed her hand over her eyes, then took the coffee from him. "I'm sorry," she said. "It's just . . . I feel as though I should be there, back at the house, helping."

Keal shook his head. "Can't risk it. You haven't felt the pull since you've been here, at the motel?"

Hours after Toria and David had found her in the Civil War world and brought her home—after thirty years of her wandering around through history—a portal had opened and tried to pull her back in. Jesse had said that spending too much time in the past made those long-ago places think she belonged to them. Time wanted her back.

Nana brushed the hair off her face and raised her eyebrows. "Nothing," she said. "I don't think it can reach this far." She placed the cup on a night table and sat on the bed.

"And that's the way we want it," Keal said. "When Dad—" He stopped himself and laughed. He'd been spending so much time with the kids, he had started thinking of Ed King, Nana's son, as "Dad."

"Ed went to see a friend who might help. When he gets home, he wants to talk to you about where you went when you were first taken and what you know about the way time shifts in the other world."

She nodded. "Of course."

Keal set the bag of bagels beside the coffee cup. He looked around the room. It was a dingy place, small and gloomy. The poor woman must be going crazy shut up in here, wondering what was happening back at the house. He said, "You haven't seen anyone? No problems?"

She smiled tightly. "No Taksidian, if that's what you mean. I tried watching the news, but my head started spinning at how much the world has changed." She picked up the cup, took off the lid, and blew on the steaming liquid. She took a sip and scrunched her face at the bitterness.

"Couldn't sleep," she said. "I kept thinking that I'd wake up and find myself in twelfth-century China or at the Alamo with Santa Anna beating at the gates or in some London street during the Black Plague . . ."

Keal sat beside her and wrapped an arm around her shoulder. "You're here, home, in your own time," he assured her. "All you need to think about right now is how great it's going to be to get to know your son again, and your grandkids. They're sweet people."

"Ah," she said, sounding as though she was already with them, basking in their attention.

"It's okay," he said. "All better now."

"No," she said, turning to look at him. A tear broke away from the corner of her eye and ran down her cheek. "It's not okay, not as long as they're in that house. Can't you feel it? It's not finished with us, not any of us."

# CHAPTER

# twenty-six

FRIDAY, 7:43 A.M.

When they stepped into the short corridor, it was empty.

"Let's go," Xander said, heading for locker 119. It was about twenty paces away from the bathroom, against the opposite wall.

David followed. Conflicting emotions left him not knowing how to feel. He was disappointed with himself for going along with Xander's plan to skip school. At the same time, he

133

was doing mental backflips over getting to seeing Young Jesse again. He couldn't think of a better person to help them figure out the house and rescue Mom—even if the younger version of Jesse had not yet spent fifty years navigating through time. He was still one of the builders of the house.

Besides, he really liked the kid. In the short time they were together the day before, David felt the bond between them grow stronger, like a muscle being flexed. David and Old Jesse had hit it off immediately in a way that could only be explained as part of the mystery of kinship—family ties, blood, and all that. Where Old Jesse could have been his grandpa, Young Jesse felt like a brother.

A man stepped out of the cafeteria doors, where the main hallway intersected with this shorter one. He walked straight into the longer corridor without turning his head.

Xander and David continued to the locker. Xander's padlock was on it from when Taksidian had tried to come through. Xander checked the locker next to it: also empty, so he shifted the lock to that one. He lifted the latch and opened the door.

"Go ahead," he said. "I'll be right behind you, so get out of the closet fast."

"What am I going to do, count the towels?" David's eyes scanned the empty locker. He remembered how frightened he'd been finding out what it did the first time. He had shut himself in the house's second-floor linen closet, planning on scaring Xander. But when he had emerged, instead of being home, he was in the school.

He stepped up into the cramped space. The metal floor buckled under his feet. He turned to tell his brother he was ready, but Xander was already slamming the door.

It was instantly dark, except for light slicing through gill-like vents in the door. These slits faded, as though someone had turned a dimmer on the school's overhead fluorescents and the sunlight streaming through the windows. David's shoulder was touching one of the locker walls; then the wall was gone. He bent his knees and held out his hands for balance as the floor became firmer and straighter. The scent in his nostrils changed from pencil shavings and rust to the sweet outdoorsiness of freshly washed sheets and towels.

The floor, then his sneakers started to glow as light poured in from under the door. When the air around him had stopped . . . *vibrating* was the best word he could think of. When it stopped vibrating, he found the handle and turned it. He stepped into the hallway outside his and Xander's bedroom.

He shut the door and waited. Sunlight from various windows caught particles of dust floating in the air. He listened—for squeaking hinges, shutting doors, footsteps, voices: any noise inconsistent with an empty house. Something creaked, and he jumped. He decided the sound had been the house groaning against a gusty wind, but his heart settled into a faster-than-normal pace.

*Fight or flight,* he thought, a term he'd learned in school. It meant that when you perceived danger or the possibility of danger, your body shifts into self-protection mode: neurons in the part of the brain responsible for physical action start firing faster—not unlike a race car revving its engine at the starting line. Adrenaline production increases, quickening your heart and making you more aware. What your body is preparing for is fight or flight, combat or escape.

David hadn't thought about it at the time, but he was certain his heart rate had picked up when Dan Rainey first confronted Xander. Then, David had been ready to fight. On the other hand, when the Berserker had attacked, David had made tracks for the portal home: flight.

During the past two weeks, he figured his adrenal glands must have squirted a decade's worth of adrenaline into his veins. He hoped they didn't wear out. He had a feeling he wasn't nearly done fighting-or-flighting.

The closet door opened, and Xander stepped out. He glanced around. "Everything okay?"

"No," David said. "But I didn't hear anything weird, if that's what you mean."

"Let's get to it," Xander said. "I'm guessing we have about an hour before Keal gets here."

CHAPTER

twenty-seven

FRIDAY, 7:39 A.M.

They walked to the far end of the second floor's main hallway, turned left, and stepped up to the wall Keal had
constructed the day before. It was unfinished, just wallboards affixed to two-by-four studs with screws. The screw
holes and seams where the wallboards touched each other
needed plastering and sanding. Then they'd have to try to
match the rest of the hall's wainscoting and wallpaper, so it

wouldn't look like a false wall, but a real one. The door, which would eventually be a "secret door," was missing altogether.

Xander and David walked through the opening. Keal had also managed to put up the second wall, the one designed for security instead of disguise. For this one, however, he had used one-inch-thick plywood slabs, not flimsy wallboard. David could tell by the placement of the screws that Keal had installed at least double the usual number of studs.

Xander rapped his knuckles against the wood. It made a solid *thunking* sound.

David moved to the opening that serviced the stairs leading to the third floor—no door here yet either. He peered at the other side of the wall. "Plywood on this side too," he said. He sandwiched the wall between his hands and tried to wiggle it. His entire body moved, but the wall didn't budge.

"That's as sturdy a wall as I've ever seen outside of castles," Xander said. "I think Keal is out to prove you wrong about these walls not being able to keep Phemus from coming into the main part of the house."

"You think this will hold him?" David said.

"Not for a second," Xander said. "But Keal's *trying*."

They stomped up the stairs and pushed the old-fashioned button that turned on the lights. The hallway lit up like the portable walkways that connected airport terminals to planes. David was struck once again by how much it looked like a turn-of-the-century hotel corridor. Six-panel wooden doors lined each side, ten doors on the left and ten on the right. Dark squares of wood lined the bottom third of the walls. Wallpaper, illustrated with vertical vines and leaves, covered the upper portion. The floor was made of polished planks with a narrow, intricately patterned rug running its length. Here and there, small tables stood against the right wall. A wall light glowed between each door.

David approached the first of these lights. It depicted an old bearded man. He wore a tunic and a wreath perched on his head. He pointed into an open book. Light flickered from his eyes and out of the top of the carving.

Xander stepped up beside him. He said, "I remember thinking that guy was Socrates or Plato."

"A teacher?" David said. "Who's that supposed to scare?"

"Students," Xander said. "Maybe they had whole classrooms coming through. Field trips to the future: does everybody have their permission slips?"

"Probably he's a god," David suggested. "And that book tells him who's supposed to die. That'd be scary."

Xander leaned closer, squinting. "It's so detailed. Think Jesse carved it?"

"If so, he missed his calling. He'd have made a fortune selling these."

Xander gave him a nudge. "Let's get looking. You take the right side." He peered into the first antechamber and shut the door. "Remember: a hammer, a nail apron, a piece of blue-print . . ."

David interrupted: "A saw, a plumb-bob, a planer thing. I know."

He went to the first door on the right. Inside, the theme of the items hanging from the hooks and resting on the bench appeared to be *torture*: a whip, a black hood cinched on the open end with a rope, a contraption that resembled a large vise—with a shape and size that made David believe it had been designed to accommodate a human head. He slammed the door, feeling like his eyes were going to pop out of their sockets.

*Never*, he thought. *You will never get me through that portal!*

He went to the next door. He'd seen the items before: binoculars, a gun belt with bullets, an empty holster, a smooth, round helmet.

He hit three antechambers containing themes he'd never seen before: something to do with a dark place (candles, matches, a coil of rope), animals (a leash, a dart pistol, one of those poles with a loop of wire at one end for ensnaring vicious beasts), and some sport (a leather ball the size of a cantaloupe, what appeared to be wooden shin-guards, a well-used club or bat).

*Hmmm* . . . He might like that one.

He continued checking behind the doors until he reached the end of the hall, then started back, opening each door a second time. He wasn't surprised to see new items in the antechambers he had looked into just minutes before, but that the rooms changed themes—and did it so quickly—never failed to fascinate him. The portals constantly shifted, some worlds vanishing, new ones appearing. Because of this, the twenty doors represented an infinite number of worlds. Well, if not *infinite*, then at least *unknowable*. One thing was certain: there were a lot of them. If there weren't, finding Mom wouldn't be nearly the challenge it was.

Xander opened and closed doors on the other side. Occasionally he'd call out what he'd found.

"Hey, here's that beach one. Remember, the first theme we found?"

"Nothing but weapons in this one, Dae. Knives, spears, swords!"

"Holy cow, I think this one's all about *pigs*. What could that world be like?"

David moved quietly from door to door until he was half-way through his fourth lap. He cracked the door open and saw the items inside. Pushing the door wide, he turned to his brother.

"Xander," he said, "come here. We're going over."

# CHAPTER

twenty-eight

Xander slammed a door and turned. "You've got it? Jesse's world?" He hurried toward David.

"Not Jesse's," David said, "but one he talked about."

Xander looked in. "The Civil War? Dae, we've already been there. A couple of times."

Four times, in fact. Believing that Mom had left a message for them on a tent, they had kept returning. But it had turned out to be Nana, Dad's mother, who'd left the message. She had been kidnapped from the house thirty years ago. She was the reason Dad had brought the family to the house in the first place. Now, Nana was back and Mom was gone.

*So much like a video game,* David thought again. But losing here meant more than hitting a reset button; here, your mom gets stolen, your arm broken, and your life threatened. That one of them wasn't already playing harps with the angels was a miracle.

"Have you forgotten how many times we almost died over there?" Xander said. "Shut the door. Forget about it." He walked away.

"Xander," David pleaded, "Jesse said we were supposed to get the doctor for that injured soldier."

Xander spun on him, arms out. "Soldiers die in war, Dae! That's the way it is. Are we supposed to go back to every war in history and save everyone?"

"No, but—"

"But what? It can't be done. Not by us, not by anyone."

"I'm not saying everyone, Xander," David said. "For whatever reason, this house is picking them for us. It's showing us places in history where we can make a difference. If what happened after I saved Marguerite is any clue, we can change history for the better, maybe save millions."

"Well," Xander said, "if that's what this is all about, let's start at the beginning. Let's go back and stop the first act of violence man committed against man. Maybe no one else will get the idea, and there'll be no wars. Ta-da, job done."

David thought about it. "Cain and Abel?"

"There you go," Xander said. "First murder. Let's go stop it, maybe convince Cain his brother's not such a bad guy. Arm-wrestle him instead. Imagine how *that* would change history."

David didn't think it would, and didn't believe Xander thought so either. Man's nature was violent. If it hadn't been Cain, it would have been someone else. And probably not long afterward. Another of Adam and Eve's children.

Xander walked to a door on his side of the hall and opened it. He pulled it closed and moved to the next.

David went into the Civil War antechamber. He looked at the items on the hooks: two military coats, a gray one and a blue one; matching military hats—*kepis;* and a sword in a scabbard. On the bench, leaning against the wall, was a Harper's Ferry rifle. It was a Union soldier who needed a doctor, so David pulled down the blue coat. He slipped his right arm into a sleeve and let the left side hang over his cast.

"What are you doing?" Xander stood in the doorway, fists pressed against his hips.

"Pulling a Xander," David said. Dad sometimes said that when one of them did something he had been told not to do.

Xander brushed past him, braced himself in front of the portal door, and crossed his arms over his chest. "I don't think so."

David snatched the blue kepi off the hook and threw it down at Xander's feet. "Cain and Abel is not one of the times in history the house has shown us," he said. "We can't choose the times, Xander, but we can decide to do something about the times we *are* shown."

"You sound like Gandalf," Xander said.

David decided to take it as a compliment. Gandalf was cool, and *The Fellowship of the Ring* was his brother's favorite movie. He smiled. "What do you say, in and out?"

Xander's shoulders slumped. "If only I had a dollar for every time we said *that*, and almost died."

David sat on the bench. "You *know* I don't like the Civil War world," he said. "Both sides took shots at me. General Grant himself did! Some soldiers tried to send *Toria* to the front line. The place—the time—doesn't *want* us. But Jesse thinks we should have done something there. All I want to do is find the doctor for that guy and get out." He gave Xander his best puppy dog look, which admittedly worked a lot better on Mom than on anyone else in the family. He said, "That's all. Please."

Xander moved away from the door to sit beside him. "The only reason to do it," he said, "is to make something better, right? How do we know if it works?"

"We'll ask Jesse," David said. "He says he 'remembers' it."

"And if nothing comes of it?" Xander said. "What if you get the doctor and nothing changes?"

David nodded. "Okay, if nothing changes, I won't insist anymore. I'll admit I don't know what we're supposed to do, who we're supposed to do it to, or how to do it." He cocked an eye at Xander. "Fair enough?"

Xander patted him on the back and stood. He picked up the kepi and handed it to David, then tugged down the gray coat.

"You're going as the Confederate?" David said.

"I can't make you do it again, can I?" He slipped into the uniform.

"How are we going to play it this time?" David said. "The soldier-prisoner thing worked the best."

"For about ten minutes," Xander said. "It's like Jesse said, the people in the times we go into sense that we don't belong. They don't like us no matter what side we're on."

David stood and shrugged out of his coat. "Trade with me," he said, holding it up for Xander.

"No, I—"

"If we're going as soldier and prisoner, you'd be more believable as a soldier. They might try to take the rifle away from *me*."

Xander peeled off the gray coat. "Let's hope we touch down close to the encampment, like last time."

CHAPTER

# twenty-nine

They didn't.

Before David's feet hit the ground, an explosion tore up the earth forty feet away. He tumbled and came to rest on his stomach. His broken arm was under him. Both it and the ribs it was pressing into began throbbing, as though the pulse of a racing heart was the soundtrack this world demanded. Dirt rained down on him.

A plume of smoke engulfed him, so thick and gray he lost

sight of the ground directly under his face. It filled his nostrils like burrs, painful and suffocating. He inhaled through his mouth and felt the pain in his lungs. He coughed and wiped his eyes on the backs of his hands. They kept leaking, and he blinked, blinked.

"Xander!" he yelled. "Where are you?"

Rifle fire, cannon fire, shouts, and screams whisked away his words like sand tossed into a hurricane.

He crawled forward, hoping to get out of the smoke. He found a body.

"Xander?"

He patted his hands over a thigh, a hip . . . a gaping wet hole. The blood was warm, fresh. He screamed and pulled his hand away. Then reached back, feeling farther up: an arm, bent unnaturally . . . shoulders . . .

"Xander?" The word not much more than a croak.

A breeze blew past, clearing the smoke. A face stared at him, eyes and mouth stretched in a wide expression of terror. Mud and blood were streaked over the forehead and cheeks, but David saw it wasn't Xander and dropped his head to the ground.

He lifted his gaze to examine his hand. Drenched in glistening crimson, with bits of grass and dirt stuck to it. He focused past his fingers to the corpse. A Union soldier. The man's knees were bent under him, as though he had dropped on the very spot he had stood. Shards had been blown into him, opening up his lower chest. Then David realized his mistake: they weren't shards that had penetrated; they were ribs that had broken and canted out.

He pushed away, retching. His stomach heaved.

He felt hands slapping his body, as he had the dead soldier's. He screamed and swatted at the hands.

"Dae! Dae! It's me!" Xander crawled beside him, dragging the rifle on the ground, and collapsed. "You okay? You hurt?"

David covered his mouth, closed his eyes. He willed himself not to throw up. When he thought he had control over his stomach, he nodded. "I'm okay."

"We're in the heat of it, Dae," Xander said. "We can't just walk out of this, a soldier and his prisoner."

"I don't want to walk," David said. "I want to *run.*"

Xander put his arm over David's back. "We're right on the front line, but I saw Union soldiers ahead of us. We're on Union ground . . . just barely."

Remembering the last time they were in this position, David said, "They're going to try to kill me. Doesn't matter if I'm a kid or you got me covered with the rifle. This close to the battle, they'll shoot anything gray."

"Then take it off," Xander said.

Little clouds and wisps of smoke drifted past.

David lifted his upper body, and Xander got the left side of the coat out from under him. He pulled his arm out of the sleeve.

Xander rolled it into a ball and threw it.

"Xander!" David said. "We need it to find the portal."

"I have enough things. Just stay with me."

David reached for his kepi, but it was already gone.

Another explosion erupted twenty feet away. Both of them covered their heads. Clumps of earth dropped down on them.

Xander pulled his arm off David. "Take off your shirt," he said.

"My . . . why?"

"It's a yellow T-shirt," Xander said. "One, it catches the eye. We don't want that. Two, if it looks like you lost your uniform, they'll accept that better than if it looks like you never had one. I think our jeans will pass for blue uniform pants."

A bullet kicked up a divot of dirt an arm's-length from David's head. Another one slammed into the ground on the other side. One whistled over them.

"I can't believe you talked me into this," Xander said. "It's the same thing all over again!"

David gave his brother a push. "It's not the same, Xander! This time we know why we're here. This time"—he pulled off his shirt, tossed it away—"we have a *purpose.*"

Xander rolled his eyes.

"If you feel that way," David said, "why did you come?"

"I'm your big brother, Dae. It's my job to protect you. Anybody who says different hasn't ever been in a position to do it."

"Thank you." David forced a smile. "So, what are we going to do?"

"Just what you said: run."

Rifle fire rippled around them. A bullet zinged past. They dropped their heads.

Keeping the side of his face pressed in the dirt, David said, "Won't they think we're running from the battle? Shoot us as deserters?"

Xander thought about it. "Not if we're wounded. Two injured soldiers trying to make it back to camp."

"What, we limp?"

"Limp, lean on each other, and . . ." Xander scooted closer to the dead Union soldier. He reached toward the wound.

"Xander, *no!*"

"His blood or ours," Xander said. "If you were dead, wouldn't you want your blood to save the lives of two innocent kids?"

"Kind of like being an organ donor, I guess," David said weakly. His stomach felt full of acid.

"Right," Xander said. He reached again.

David grabbed his arm. "Just blood," he said. "Don't be gross."

"Just blood," Xander agreed. "That's gross enough."

David closed his eyes. Xander moved around beside him. He felt his brother's hand on his face. Wet stickiness. A coppery smell. He moaned through tight lips.

"Just a second, David," Xander said. He moved again, reaching. Then his hand pressed against David's temple and ear. "One more touch," Xander said, moving again. "Tilt up on your side." When he did, Xander's hand rubbed over his ribs. "Okay," Xander said. "Stay like that."

He stretched toward the soldier again, and David knew he was giving himself wounds.

"What about my cast?" David said.

"It's pretty much covered by the Ace bandage," Xander said. "Looks like it could have been wrapped here."

A thick drop of liquid ran down David's cheek, heading for the corner of his mouth. He smeared it away. He moaned again and said, "Xander, I can't do this!"

"You can, Dae! Open your eyes."

Xander was staring straight at him, his eyes blazing. A thick coat of blood ran down one side of his face from hairline to jaw.

David bit his lip.

"We're going to get out of this," Xander said. "If you have to think about the blood, this is what you think: that man is saving our lives."

David nodded.

Smoke billowed over them. Gunshots, cannons, explosions continued—had never stopped.

Xander said, "Let's go!" With that, he rose, slung the rifle over his shoulder, and reached down for David.

Arm in arm, leaning on each other, David and Xander fell into a hobbling, quick-paced gait. The Union soldiers heading for the front stared at them, more fearful than sympathetic. More than one bayed like a dog at them. David thought it was an army or regiment thing, something like the modern-day marines' "Oorah!"

They crested a hill and saw the camp. Same one they'd visited before: two long rows of large tents, separated by a wide central aisle. Soldiers either stood in small groups in the aisle and on this side of the encampment, or streamed toward the boys.

"Do we act wounded now?" David asked.

Xander released his hold on David to walk a little straighter. He maintained a limp, though it was less pronounced. "Let's be a little *less* wounded," he said, wiping away some of the blood on his face. "If we look like we've already been beat up pretty bad, maybe they'll leave us alone."

As they approached, a few soldiers broke out of their groups to meet them.

Xander held up his hand. "We're fine." He groaned, just to let them know they weren't *too* fine. To David he whispered, "I don't know if they used terms like *okay* or *all right.*"

"*Fine's* fine," David said. "I think."

Two soldiers ran up to them. One grabbed David by the arm. The other snatched the rifle off Xander's back.

"Hey," Xander said.

"Just holding it for you, boy," the soldier said. He hooked an arm around Xander's back.

The one gripping David's arm eased up. "Sorry," he said. "Thought you were going to fall." He shifted his hands, carefully trying to find a way of supporting David without injuring him further. He leaned forward to get a better glimpse at his wounds.

"Have you been shot?" he asked.

"I don't know what happened," David answered. "I was playing my drum, then—*this.*"

"Cannon, most probable," the soldier said. He released David long enough to grab a blanket from the ground and throw it over David's shoulders. It was about as soft as tree bark and itched his skin.

Passing the first of the tents, the man yelled out, "Doctor! We need a doctor!"

"No, no," Xander said. "We are not as injured as others. See after them first. Please, just set us down near one of the hospital tents."

The soldiers looked across David and Xander at each other. They helped them to a series of stones arranged outside a tent. The stones were the size of half watermelons, and David realized this was the Civil War version of a waiting room. He and Xander moaned and groaned appropriately as the soldiers eased them down.

"Thank you," Xander said, and David nodded.

The soldier who helped Xander stood and hitched up his pants. He pulled the rifle off his back and extended it to Xander, then pulled it back. He hefted it, moved it in his hands, as though something about it puzzled him. He eyed it, stock to barrel, frowning.

"Sir," Xander said, holding out his hand.

The soldier handed him the rifle. He said, "Have I seen you boys before?"

David lowered his head, pretending to be weak from his injuries. If anyone recognized them from their previous visits, they would be in big trouble. Each time, they had run away, guns blasting at them.

"Maybe," Xander said, also turning his face away—he had opted to become suddenly interested in a glob of blood on his thigh. "Don't know."

"Hmm . . ." the soldier said. He walked away without another word. His compatriot, who had helped David, fell in beside him. Their heads leaned toward each other, indicating that they were sharing their thoughts about the wounded young men.

"Something I said, or suspicion because we don't belong?" Xander said.

"The rifle, maybe. Is it pulling toward the portal?"

Xander balanced it across both palms. The gun shifted suddenly, and he closed his fingers around it. "Yeah," he said, "a little."

David stood. He adjusted the blanket over his shoulders and gripped the edges over his chest. He glanced toward the soldiers. Two more had joined them, and they were watching the boys.

He pretended to help Xander stand. "Let's find the doctor and get out of here."

# thirty-one

"Try this one." Xander pointed his thumb at the tent with the waiting room stones.

David flipped open the flap. Four soldiers sat or lay on tables. One of them was getting his arm stitched. A nurse tugged at the thread. She stopped to address David. "Life threatening?"

"No, sorry." He backed out. "Come on," he told Xander. He went to the next tent and peeked in. A man was sitting on a cot, slipping a leg into a pair of pants. David said, "Excuse me."

From outside the next tent in line, he heard a man screaming. He turned to Xander, who was watching the soldiers at the head of the camp. "This is it!"

"Hurry."

David pushed through. A man lay on a table, convulsing. Blood jutted from a wound in his neck. His screams became gurgles. A woman in a nurse's hat and blood-covered smock pressed a cloth to another injury in the man's chest. She looked up quickly.

"Boy!" she yelled. "You must fetch Dr. Scott. Two tents down. Hurry!" Her head gestured toward the rear of the camp.

"Got it!" he said, and ran out. He hooked right and shot to the second tent over. He threw open the flap and stomped in. "Dr. Scott!" he yelled.

Men occupied six cots. Bandages covered various parts of their bodies. A nurse knelt close to one. She was holding a spoon to his lips and whispering to him. Her back was to David, but something about her sent an icy-footed centipede scampering up his spine. He froze in place, watching her try to coax the man into taking a bite.

"Dr. Scott is not here!"

The woman's voice jarred David out of his trance. Another nurse sat on a cot on the opposite side. She held a folded cloth to a patient's head and was staring at David.

He said, "But . . . we *need* him!"

"He left ten minutes ago," the nurse said. "I don't know where he went."

He pushed out of the tent.

"Can we go now?" Xander said.

"He wasn't there," David said. He ran back to the tent with the severely injured soldier.

"He's not there!" he yelled at the nurse. "Where is he?"

"I don't know!" She closed her eyes and shook her head. When her eyes opened, they pierced David. "Try his quarters," she said. "Last tent on the left."

He spun out of the tent. The blanket snagged on the flap and slipped off his shoulders. He didn't stop to retrieve it.

Behind him, the nurse yelled, "Tell him it's Major Rawlins!"

Xander grabbed his arm. "Don't run," he said, and looked toward the front of the camp. A group of about ten soldiers had gathered. All of them had eyes turned on the boys.

"Great," David said. "Stay here so it doesn't look like we're escaping." As fast as he dared, he walked to the last tent on the other side. "Dr. Scott?" he said and pushed the flap aside. A man with a trimmed silver beard rested on a cot. A bloody smock lay crumpled on the dirt floor next to him. His left arm was draped over his eyes.

He said, "Go away."

"Your nurse wants you," David said. "A man is dying. He needs you."

"Find Dr. Jacobs," Dr. Scott said.

"It's Major Rawlins."

The arm flew off his face so fast, David didn't see it happen. Dr. Scott rolled off the cot and pushed past David. "Where?" he said, running. "Where?"

"There! There!" David said, running with him. "See Xan— I mean, where that boy is standing?"

The doctor beelined it for Xander.

David stopped. He suddenly felt sick. His stomach tumbled freely inside his body. A gray cloud narrowed his vision, and he became dizzy. He dropped to his knees and fell forward, catching himself with his one good arm. He closed his eyes. A montage of images flashed in his head: faces, maps, newspaper headlines, scenes of violence and bloodshed, war . . . a bearded man on horseback taking a bullet to the chest and falling off . . .

"David!" Xander yelled. He lifted David by his shoulders. "You all right? What's the matter?"

David put his hand over his eyes. The images faded until only blackness remained. He opened his eyes, blinked. His vision came back. "Dizzy," he said.

"Can you run?" Xander asked.

"Run?"

Xander pointed. The group of soldiers had grown to fifteen or more. They were marching down the camp's center aisle, headed directly for them. At the head of the pack was the man he had imagined seeing shot off his horse: Ulysses S. Grant.

CHAPTER

# thirty-two

"You!" Grant shouted, pointing at David and Xander. "Stop right there!"

"Go, go, go!" Xander yelled, shoving David.

David stumbled. His vision blurred, then cleared. Xander dashed past him and stopped. He extended his hand to David, who grabbed it, and they ran.

A dozen voices rose up behind them: "There they go!" "Stop!" "Spies!"

David waited for the first shot, wondered if it would sail harmlessly by or rip a fist-sized hole through his body.

They swung around the last tent, Dr. Scott's, and beat it for the woods—a hundred yards away at the far side of a field.

David stumbled again. He stayed up only because Xander had a firm grip on his hand.

Xander looked back. "What's wrong with you?"

"I don't know," David said. "I feel like I just woke up. I can't think straight."

Looking ahead, Xander said, "Snap out of it! If you don't, we're dead."

David inhaled, exhaled. He scanned the ground ahead of them for obstacles. He felt the muscles in his legs working— no burn yet—his feet touching down, lifting up, shooting forward.

*Here we go,* he thought. *Welcome back, David.*

The soldiers' angry voices reached him. He glanced back. They had rounded Dr. Scott's tent and were running. Two in the lead stopped to aim their rifles.

"They're going to shoot, Xander!" David hollered. "Jag left. I'll go right."

Xander released David's hand and made a sharp jog left. David mirrored the move in the other direction.

The rifles rang out, two in quick succession.

Xander veered right. David swung left and they crossed paths, Xander just ahead of David.

"Keep doing it," David said.

Another shot. Bark exploded from a tree fifty yards ahead.

"You got all the items, Xander," David reminded him. "Are they pulling?"

"Oh yeah," Xander said. "Way off to the left, but let's get into the woods first."

They zigged and zagged, pushed harder.

Three more gunshots . . . another two. David heard a bullet fly past.

"Here," Xander said. He held the rifle out behind him without looking. "For the pull," he said. "Don't try to shoot it. It'll just slow you down."

"Wait!" David said. He reached for it, touched it, and Xander let go. Instead of falling back into David's hand, it spun forward and shot diagonally away from them.

"Hey!" Xander said.

"It just took off," David said. "Should we go after it?"

Behind them, a soldier fired.

"No way," Xander said. "The woods—ten seconds away. That thing's not even close, cutting across the field like that. It was heading straight for the portal."

Xander leaped over a bush and practically vanished in the shadows of the woods. David plowed in, no leaping necessary. They continued to put distance between themselves and the soldiers. They swerved around trees, hurdled bushes, crunched over twigs.

David threw a look back. The field was fifty yards behind them. The soldiers pressed on, but had not yet hit the tree line. He slowed and stopped.

"Xander!" he called.

David bent over and put his hands on his knees. He panted. He dropped to his knees, then onto his side. The ground-cover prickled his bare skin. He filled his lungs over and over. He closed his eyes, wondering if he'd be assaulted by the images again. They didn't come, but he did feel lightheaded.

He remembered learning in school about Grant's death in the Civil War. When would that be? How many days or years from now did that happen? Wait a minute: it never happened. Grant survived the Civil War and became the eighteenth president of the United States, after Andrew Johnson—David had to memorize the presidents in order in sixth grade. And he had always liked Grant: he was considered one of the best military commanders ever. Plus he was the president who controlled James West and Artemus Gordon in the *Wild Wild West* TV show.

But it was so clear in his memory: Grant died in battle in—he knew this—1862. That's right, toward the beginning of the war, which ended in 1875. No! That wasn't right. The war ended in 1865. He'd memorized a poem about it:

*In 1861 the war begun*
*In 1862 the bullets flew*

*In 1863 Lincoln set slaves free*
*In 1864 there still was a war*
*In 1865 hardly a man is still alive*

There were no more lines, no more years of war.

*Memory.* He *remembered* Grant having died in 1862, at the Battle of Shiloh, and the war lasting until 1875.

Xander's feet crunched over the ground, moving quickly toward him, then stopped. "Dae," he whispered. "Dae!"

When David looked up, Xander was sitting with his back against a tree. He glanced around the tree toward the soldiers. He cast wide eyes at David. "David! They're coming."

David popped his head up. The soldiers had reached the tree line. Grant was twenty feet behind. He was swinging a pointing hand, positioning the soldiers an equal distance apart. Finding Xander and David was going to be an organized affair.

David rolled to a tree and sat up behind it. He said, "Xander, it worked. We changed history. I remember the way it was—and the way it is. Like Jesse. That must be why I felt sick and got dizzy. My memories were colliding. It happened right when I sent Dr. Scott to the tent, to Major Rawlins."

Xander stared at David for a good ten seconds. David could see the wheels turning in his head. Finally he said, "We don't have time for this." He popped his head around the tree, pulled it back quickly. "They're in the woods."

"Just tell me," David said. "I *have* to know. I need know for sure which of my memories are the *right* ones. You know, history as it is now, right now. When did the Civil War end?"

Without hesitating Xander said, "1865."

"Did Grant die in the war?"

"David!"

"Please!"

"Your father has been a history teacher your whole life, until this year, and you ask something like that?" He sighed. "No, he became president after the war, in 1869. Now come on! Your pasty skin is going to be like a beacon for those guys." He pushed himself up the tree until he was standing.

David looked down at his shirtless chest. He had forgotten. The blood Xander had smeared on his ribs had dried; it looked liked crusty ketchup. He turned toward the tree and stood. "One last thing," he said.

"If we don't move now," Xander said, exasperated, "I'm going to lose the coat and kepi—*and* those guys are going to shoot us."

David shot a glance at the soldiers. They apparently thought their quarry had gone to ground as soon as they hit the woods. They were moving slowly, kicking at clumps of leaves and twigs, bayoneting bushes. He darted from his tree to Xander's. No one yelled.

Xander's coat was fluttering, as though caught in gale-force winds, in the direction they had to travel. The kepi vibrated against his tight grip.

Dae looked up at him. "How many people died in the war?"

Xander pressed his lips together. David knew his brother wanted to deck him.

"Six hundred thousand," Xander said. "Give or take."

"Xander," David said, excited. "I remember this—reading it, writing it, seeing it in a documentary, Mrs. Felton putting it on the whiteboard: the Civil War took over *two million* lives. If what you're saying is true, that only six hundred thousand died, then we just saved . . ." He calculated. "We just saved one million, four hundred thousand people!"

# CHAPTER

# thirty-three

FRIDAY, 8:52 A.M.

Jesse's eyes sprang open. They jittered in their sockets, but he did not see the ceiling above his hospital bed, only the dream that had awakened him. Not a dream as much as a dream of memories. When history changed—whether at his hands or another's—the events that had lost their place in time flooded his mind, the way a lightbulb briefly flares with intensity before blowing its filament. He liked to think

168

of it as history-that-is-no-longer-history saying, "I was here! I was . . ." *Gone.*

He never pursued *why* changed history uttered this last gasp or why *he* could sense it. He simply accepted it as the way the universe worked, a part of who he was. But he knew in his heart what it was all about. It was God's way of telling him, *You matter. This is why you're here.*

Florescent lights above him flickered on, penetrating his eyes and dimming the images of a history that never was. He still remembered them and would continue to remember for a few hours most likely. But as life encroached and time passed, they would become like a movie projected in a theater whose house lights grew progressively brighter, until the image on the screen vanished in the glare of reality.

He became aware of the EKG machine, like his heart's radio station. Currently it was playing a quick-tempo'd oldie-but-goodie: *beep-beep, beep-beep, beep-beep.* The machine added another tone, designed to alert listeners when the station was getting too jazzy for its own good: *wa-wa-wa-wa-wa-wa!* Boring and irritating, in Jesse's opinion.

A nurse leaned over him. "Mr. Wagner?" She stared into his face, then turned and flicked the radio station off, severing the alarm in mid-*wa!*

"Finally," he said, surprised by the frailty of his voice.

"Are you all right?" she said. "Your heart got a little excited there."

*Well, of course it did,* he thought. *History changed. Things just got better—and almost nobody knows it.*

Whenever it happened, his heart always raced. He didn't know if it was an emotional response from the excitement of witnessing a phenomenal event or if it was biological, the body pumping blood to the brain so it could process the clash of memories—the memories of current history tossing out the memories of history-that-is-no-longer-history. At least his body had acclimated to the assaults. No more nausea. No more dizziness. No more grogginess, as though the mind was too preoccupied with watching that brief, final flare of history to handle life as well.

He wondered if one or more of the new gatekeepers possessed this ability. He hoped for their sake they did. It was a dormant trait, like a recessive gene, that was activated only through time travel. Even then, in some people—he thought of his brother, Aaron—it took years to kick in; in others it came quickly. He had his first flash of history-that-is-no-longer-history after his third time "going over."

He smiled. *Going over* was another term from the King kids. His father—and subsequently he himself—had called it *jaunting.* Didn't matter—the only thing that did matter was that they were doing it. The memories now battling it out in his head proved they not only were jaunting, but that they had taken his advice: they were making a difference.

*Way to go, boys,* he thought. *I knew you could do it.*

"Well, it looks like everything's all right," the nurse said. "Just a little scare. Were you dreaming?"

"Oh, was I," he said. He tried to smile, but wasn't sure he managed one. He lifted a shaking hand, feeling the tug of IV lines like a leash. "Please . . ."

She cupped his hand in both of hers and lowered it to the bed. "What is it?" she said.

Sweet girl.

"I used to record my dreams," he said slowly, "but I believe I can't do it this time. Could you . . ." He could feel it now, his smile. "Could you write it down for me? I'll tell you."

"Uh . . ." she said, frowning.

*Of course, she was busy.*

Then she grinned and nodded. "Yeah, sure. I'll just go get a pen and paper." She hurried away.

When he was younger, Jesse spent countless hours in the house's library, reading, learning, absorbing biographies, philosophy, science. But mostly, history. It had not been merely an intellectual pursuit, not when his life revolved around traveling to different times—"worlds," as the King kids would say. He had found that the more he understood about the worlds he traveled to, the better his chance at accomplishing the mission he had been handed; the better his chances for survival. For him, cracking a book in his library was as crucial to his life as picking up a gun at a firing range was for a police officer or soldier.

The nurse returned, pad and pencil in hand. She dragged a chair across the room, positioning it beside him. She settled in and said, "Go ahead."

He started: "Ulysses S. Grant died on April 7, 1862."

She brightened. "Oh, an alternate history story. I love those."

He winked at her and continued. "Earlier that day, Grant's close friend and aide-de-camp John Aaron Rawlins sustained fatal wounds from Confederate snipers. Upon learning of Rawlins's death, Grant flew into a fit of rage. He mounted his horse and charged to the front lines, where the very same snipers killed him . . ."

# thirty-four

Xander gripped David's shoulder and peered around the tree. "Ready?" he said.

"Let's do it."

Xander smiled. "That's what I want to hear. Follow me." He broke from the cover of the tree, running parallel to the tree line.

David leaped in behind him.

Soldiers yelled. A rifle cracked, and a branch shattered in

front of them. A piece of flying wood struck his arm. He yelled, grabbed his bicep, didn't slow.

Xander did, turning to check on David.

David crashed into him. They tumbled, rolling over leaves and twigs that poked and sliced David's back. "Go!" he said, grunting out the word. He felt Xander struggling under his legs, saw him reaching for the kepi, which rolled away from his hand and wedged itself into a bush. It ripped through the bush and sailed away.

Xander scrambled up. He lifted David, and they were off again—hurdling bushes, dodging trees, ducking under branches.

Someone fired. A sound like a bat striking a tree came from right behind David. Another shot. Another. Between the loud cracks, David could hear the men stomping through the woods after them, yelling, calling out instructions to one another.

*Wouldn't that be nice?* David thought. *Grant kills the boy who saved his life!* He didn't know how helping Major Rawlins ultimately led to saving Grant, but he knew it did. Grant and over a million others.

Xander fell into a bush, rolled through it, and was running again before David caught up.

"Just ahead," Xander yelled. "Has to be."

They were close to the spot in the woods where the rifle would have ended up, had it continued its trajectory when

David had watched it spin through the field. He could tell by how tight Xander's uniform coat was on his back that it was pulling him forward.

Movement caught David's eye. Ahead of them and off to the left, more soldiers plowed into the woods. They had obviously come from the front of the camp and were moving to cut the boys off—or get them in a crossfire with the soldiers behind them.

"Xander!"

"I see them!"

Then David spotted it: the portal. It was ahead of them on the right. Its edges were indistinct, but it appeared to be less door-shaped than he was used to; this one was more like an elongated egg. Its rippling presence—like heated air—distorted the trees and bushes behind it. As he watched, it wavered and moved, appearing to slip farther to the right and rise.

"I see it," David said.

"Where?"

"To your right," David said. "You're going to pass it!"

"No," Xander said. "The coat—"

Shots rang out from the new soldiers. So close now. Another shot came from behind. Setting up the crossfire.

David veered out of Xander's path. He ran straight for the portal.

"David!" Xander said behind him. "Wait!"

David turned. "Come on! It's right here!"

Xander's coat fluttered and tugged—pointing close to the portal, but not right at it. If the portal was at the twelve o'clock position on a watch face, the coat wanted to go to eleven o'clock. The soldiers were at six o'clock and nine o'clock— converging on the brothers, who David supposed were directly in the center.

Xander pointed. "The coat says that way."

"Look—!" David turned. The portal had shifted again. "The portal's moving. The coat's just not keeping up with it. Come on!" He ran for the portal and heard Xander fall in behind him.

More yells from the soldiers. More gunfire.

David reached the shimmering oval, squeezed his eyes shut, and leaped.

As a foul smelling breeze blew out of the portal, instantly turning David's stomach, Xander yelled, "Nooooo—!"

# thirty-five

David came down hard on the floor and rolled into a wall. Xander tumbled behind him.

*That smell*—*!* David thought, gagging in his throat and in his mind. He opened his eyes: a gray stone wall—similar to the chamber Taksidian's pantry had sent him into. But this one was stained and filthy with muck. And here the darkness wasn't complete; faint light flickered, making shadows jitter around on the wall.

He rolled over. Xander was lying on the floor, pushed up

on one arm. His shocked eyes moved between two items that chilled David's blood as surely as the Atlantic Ocean had done: High up on one wall a wide, rusty pair of shackles dangled from chains. On the floor below, another pair rested on coils of metal links. The shackles were hinged open, like twin serpents frozen in midbite.

The brothers were in a room about ten feet square, with stone walls on three sides. The fourth side was open, except for a grid of thick, flat lengths of metal that formed the bars of a prison cell. In the dark cloud of despair that was seeping into his consciousness, David felt a tinge of hope: the cell door was open.

A couple of matches' worth of flames sputtered atop a torch leaning out from a wall beyond the bars.

"This *isn't* the antechamber," David said.

Xander's mouth opened, but nothing came out. He squinted at the shackles and bars, as though he suspected someone of pulling an elaborate joke on them.

David pushed closer to his brother. He held his nose, said, "What is that *smell?*" It was like a litterbox that hadn't been changed—*ever*. Mingled with that was something else, something worse. David remembered a few years before when the family had spent a weekend with friends in San Diego. They'd come home to find that the refrigerator motor had gone out, spoiling hamburger and milk and leftover chili. *This* smelled like that had, the stench of decay.

Xander scurried up and crouched in front of David. He

grabbed David's arm. "The portal in the house didn't bring us here. I don't know how to get home," he whispered. Panic made his voice high, his words fast.

"Can't—" David said. His eyes scanned over the Union army coat. "Won't the coat show us the way?"

Xander pulled the front of it away from his chest, let it fall back. "It's not doing anything now. What if the items don't work when they're not in the world they belong to?"

"But—" David's mouth had suddenly dried up. "We *have* to get home. Xander, we have to!"

Xander nodded. "We'll . . . we'll figure something out."

They stood, and Xander walked to the bars.

Just then, a siren wailed—*no, no*, David thought. *Not a siren!* It was a *person* screaming, a long wrenching howl of agony.

Xander grabbed a bar, as if to steady himself.

The scream stretched longer than a single breath, with barely a pause for the guy to pull in another. It echoed against the walls and was joined by more voices. They moaned and cried, the way a barking dog can set off a chain of baying and yapping neighborhood pets.

David slowly squatted. He wanted to shrink within himself and disappear.

Xander stepped backward away from the bars. He bumped into David, pulled him up by the arm, then shuffled him into a corner of the cell where the shadows were darkest. He said, "I'm officially creeped out."

"Let's . . . not move," David whispered. He thought if he ran into the screamer or whatever was *making* him scream, he'd faint on the spot and wake up screaming himself.

"This is the last place we should be," Xander said. "If we're stuck in this world—"

"Don't say that!"

Xander snapped up his hand, gesturing for David to calm down, be cool. "We're here now," Xander continued, "maybe just for a little bit . . . maybe longer. Either way, there's gotta be a better place to wait it out than this."

David lowered his gaze. He said, "I'm sorry."

"For what?"

"Going in the wrong portal." David's voice was trembling. "I just thought . . . I mean, I *really* thought that was it."

Xander shook his head. "It's not your fault. We've never seen two portals before. And those soldiers . . . *Man!* I would have done the same thing."

"No, you wouldn't have." But he appreciated his brother saying it.

"Besides," Xander said, "think about what we're learning. We always wondered how Mom went in one door and out another, right? And Nana said she moved around from world to world. But until now, we'd only gone over from the house and right back to it."

David thought about it. "We still don't know how people *find* the other portals. We just stumbled on it."

"Who says they don't? Or maybe it's easy to figure out once you know what to look for." Xander stopped to listen. The screaming had faded away, leaving only the crying and muttering of a dozen different voices. He squeezed David's shoulder. "I have a feeling knowing about the other portals is going to help us find Mom."

"Sure," David said. "If we ever get back home."

Xander's expression matched the dread David felt. Still, he expected his brother to say something like, *Of course we will!*—if not for David's sake, then for his own. But Xander just cocked his head toward the cell door and whispered, "Come on."

CHAPTER

# thirty-six

The passage ran in both directions. Cells lined one side of the corridor, a wall lined the other. Torches spaced twenty or thirty feet apart did little to dispel the dismal darkness. Black shadows clung to corners, the backs of cells, the ceiling, like creatures waiting for the unsuspecting to pass too closely.

Xander grabbed the torch outside their cell and slipped it up through rings mounted to the wall. He swished the fire one direction, then the other. Both ways looked the same to

David. The glow of the other torches became dots as they stretched farther away.

"Right or left?" Xander said.

"What are we looking for?"

"A way out."

The scream rose up again, seeming to roll at them from the passage to the right like a gusty wind. Without a word, the brothers started walking the other direction. At each cell, Xander held the torch close to the bars. The first half dozen were either empty or contained piles of rags that may or may not have been prisoners. The boys addressed each pile with a "Hey" or "Hello?" but the rags didn't reply.

In the seventh cell, a boy of about thirteen cowered in a corner. Rags covered his body; a mop of dirty, shaggy hair exploded from his head. Big eyes blinked at the torch's flame.

"He's just a kid," Xander said.

"Do you speak English?" David asked.

*Blink. Blink.*

David ached for him. He grabbed the cell door and yanked on it: *Clang!*

"Yow!" Xander said, nudging David. "Shhh."

David pulled again: *Clang! Clang!*

The boy blinked.

A voice called from the direction of the scream: "*wer ist, dass oben fungierend?*"

About thirty yards away, the outline of an opening in the

wall became apparent as a torch approached from within that perpendicular passage.

*"Ich sagte, wem Mühe verursacht?"* Much closer.

"Now you've done it," Xander whispered. He took off, hurrying away from the voice and light.

David stayed right behind him, watching over his shoulder as the opening became brighter. Light spilled out of it, catching the bars on the other side.

Xander vanished into another passage on his right. Apparently, hallways were connected to this passage all along the wall. David glanced back and froze. A figure stood *right there*, not far from the cell in which they had entered this world. The torch in his hand blazed bonfire bright. David could only hope that the silhouetted man was looking the other way, or that the glare of his fire made seeing beyond its reach impossible.

He darted into the connecting hallway.

Xander was moving away, the torch tracking his progression and silhouetting his body, the way the bigger torch had done the other man. The light stopped moving.

"David, come on," Xander whispered.

David glanced around the corner. The man was near now. He was standing in front of the boy's cell. David thought the kid must be the only prisoner in this section. How else would the guy know to go right to him? He hoped that meant there weren't many kids—or many people no matter their age—locked up like this.

The man yelled into the cell. *"Berühren Sie die Tür wieder, Kind, und ich komme für Sie zunächst!"* He slammed his palm into the bars—*clang!*—and turned to return the way he had come.

The boy began to weep.

"David!"

He ran to catch up.

They found other passages lined with cells, and more prisoners, all adults. Most shied away from David and Xander, covering their faces or scurrying into corners. Some began crying; others yelled out, causing the boys to hurry away and dart into the first intersecting passage they came to. Before long, David had no idea where they were in relation to where they'd begun or in which direction they were heading.

He touched Xander to stop him. "I think we're going in circles."

The screaming kicked up again—close.

Xander began walking toward the sound. David grabbed his shirt. "What are you doing?"

"Checking it out," Xander whispered. "Maybe the only way out is up this way. These cells, all these passageways, they're probably set in the back, away from the entrance."

"But—" David knew his eyes were buggy with terror.

"Just a look," Xander reassured him.

They moved toward the scream.

# CHAPTER

# thirty-seven

David and Xander maneuvered through the gloomy passage-ways, following the screams. David found himself lifting one arm, then the other—backstroking the tension away. But it wasn't working.

As they got closer, David realized the screamer was not alone in his suffering. Someone was moaning loudly. Another cried and mumbled words David didn't understand.

They rounded a corner and found themselves in a passageway that ended in a bright rectangle of light. Xander pressed himself against a wall and scooted closer to the doorway. David crept along behind. Slowly the room beyond came into view. It was a huge chamber, octagonal in shape, with granite-block walls. Stone supports arched up to an oval ceiling, like the rotunda at the Los Angeles City Hall, which David had seen on a fifth-grade field trip. Tall pillars outlined a smaller circle at the center of the room. On each burned a trio of heavy-duty torches; a huge fire pit, situated at the room's dead center, added its light, casting a golden glow over the entire area.

It looked like the sort of place city councils would meet, or senators, or even celebrities and other lah-de-dah people looking for a party. What it was, however, was something much more repulsive. David recognized some of the equipment scattered around the room: an iron maiden, in which people were placed to be impaled by hundreds of spikes lining the interior; a giant spoked wheel, on which poor souls would be strapped and crushed as it rolled; and a table with a contraption on one end used for crushing legs. He'd seen all these devices on a History Channel show called *Tools of Torture in the Middle Ages*.

David turned away. He tried to slow his breathing, but he couldn't do anything about his heart trying to pound its way out of his chest.

This close, the moans and cries were continuous. They were horrible to hear, worse than all of the cuts and bruises, the near-drowning and broken arm he had suffered in the other worlds—including his own. That brought to mind Taksidian, the most wicked person he had ever met. And yet, this was a *world* of Taksidians, of people who thought like him, people who enjoyed cruelty the way he did.

David grabbed Xander's arm and pulled him away from the doorway, back into the dark passage.

"It's a torture chamber!" he whispered, grinding his teeth.

"Shhh!" Xander said, checking over his shoulder. "I saw the torturer. He's pacing around a guy on a rack—you know, one of those things that pull you in opposite directions until your bones and muscles—"

David slapped his hand over Xander's mouth. "I *know* what the rack is! Xander, we're stuck in *this* world, in *this* place? *We're* going to end up on that rack, I know it. I . . . I . . . can't even *look* at those things out there."

That show on TV had given him nightmares. His father had said the only explanation for atrocities like torture was summed up in one word: *evil.* There was no logic to justify it, no chalking it up to misguided principles or necessity for a greater good. It was evil, plain and simple. Dad had pointed out that the use of torture chambers, such as during the Spanish Inquisition and at the Tower of London, was only one example of human evil. History was deeply scarred by it: slavery, the Holocaust, the genocides in Rwanda and Darfur.

From the lighted room came another awful sound: *click-click-click*—the rack tightening! Its victim screamed in agony.

The others raised their mournful voices as well, as if encouraged or doubly agonized by their fellow sufferer.

David slammed his hands over his ears, squeezed his eyes shut. All he could think about were the human beings in there: perhaps a dad who had laughingly tossed his toddler in the air just days ago . . . a man sweating under the scorching sun to feed his family . . . the children they had been, never dreaming that such horrors awaited them.

"I can't take it," he said.

Xander grabbed his shoulders. "Dae, there's a staircase on the far side of the room. Want to make a break for it? We'll wait till the guy's back is turned and go for it."

David nodded, moving his head up and down in big, exaggerated motions. He heard Xander move away, and when he opened his eyes, his brother was already at the doorway, peering around the corner. He signaled for David to get up next to him.

"Hold on . . . hold on . . ." Xander whispered. His torch was on the floor, where it sputtered and smoked, ready to go out. Then Xander said, "Let's go." He stepped out of the passageway into the room, tiptoeing fast. David followed. At the far right of the large chamber, a man was turned away from them. He appeared to be whispering into the ear of another man. This other man was lying on a table, his arms pulled above his head with ropes that were attached to a wheel. Another rope-and-wheel device bound his ankles. Sweat glistened all over his body, and he was twisting his head back and forth.

David focused on Xander's back, on a smudge of dirt on the Union army coat. They were heading for an opening in the wall opposite the passage. A wide staircase rose out of sight. A moan reached him. He looked up and saw a large iron cage suspended from the ceiling. Bony, bloody fingers clutched the bars. Bare feet pressed against the bars on the bottom. Between hands and feet, rags shifted and trembled.

*Click.* The man on the rack screamed.

David couldn't help himself: he had to look. The tortured man's body was vibrating like a strummed guitar string. His head rotated sideways until his cheek touched the table, then went the other direction, only to come back again. Over and over, fast. All the while, he screamed. Then the screaming turned into heavy panting. David realized the man was staring directly at him. The man squinted, as if unable to believe his eyes.

David raised his finger to his lips, but would this man, obviously in some culture and time far removed from David's, know the symbol to be quiet? Would he care? He stopped walking, frozen in the man's gaze.

The man's face softened. His agony changed to sadness. Tears spilled out of his eyes.

The fear that had filled David's chest since seeing the torture chamber also changed, replaced by a deep ache. He wanted to help the man, but there was nothing he could do.

David was certain that any second the torturer would turn to see what the man was looking at. Then they'd *have* to run—with much less advantage than they'd had before being spotted. He wished the suffering man would turn away, not just so David and Xander wouldn't be seen, but also—mostly—because David couldn't stand seeing all that sadness on one face. And David found he couldn't look away either; that would be too much like not caring.

Then the torturer leaned sideways, blocking the man's face from view. He reached out to a handle and pulled it. *Click.* The screaming started again.

David took a step and bumped into Xander, who was backing up toward him. David gave his brother a push: *Go!*

But Xander stood firm. He pointed at the bottom hem of the Union coat. It was bent up, quivering like an old man's finger, pointing back the way they had come.

David looked into Xander's eyes. He mouthed the words, *Is it the pull?*

Xander nodded.

David looked back at the dark passageway. *Wouldn't you know?*

Slowly, the brothers began retracing their steps toward the catacombs of jail cells.

# thirty-eight

As he approached the passage, David expected to hear a sharp yell from the torturer. But then he and Xander were out of the chamber, engulfed by the shadows and chill of the tunnel-like passageway. Xander picked up speed, nearly running straight back away from the chamber. The screams dimmed as they distanced themselves from the suffering—*physically* distanced themselves anyway, David thought. His heart felt like it had remained in the chamber, aching for that poor man.

Xander braked hard, causing David to collide into him.

"We passed it," Xander said. "There." He pointed behind them at an intersecting passage. He brushed by David and darted into it. Cells opened up on either side of them. From some of them came a variety of noises: coughs, moans, crying. But as he rushed past, David didn't see any of the prisoners, just shadows.

Xander stopped in front of a cell.

David peered between the bars and saw the portal, glimmering like the disturbed surface of a pond against the back wall.

Xander grabbed at the cell door. It swung out toward them. "Let's go," he said, stepping in.

David didn't move. He was remembering the end of a conversation he'd had with Dad about torture: "Dae," Dad had told him, "a wise man once said, 'All that is necessary for evil to succeed is that good men do nothing.' That means you have to recognize it and then choose to do something to stop it."

"Come on!" Xander said. He was standing so close to the portal, his hair whipping around in the wind coming from it. "What are you doing?"

David glanced down the passage. "I have to go back," he said.

"What?" Xander came out of the cell and reached for him.

David backed away. "Xander, that man . . . the guy on the rack. We can't just leave him."

Xander shook his head. "What are you talking about? We

don't belong here. What's happening to him happened already, years ago, maybe centuries ago."

"It's happening now."

"Dae, there's nothing we can do." He waved his hand. "The portal's *right here!*" He stepped toward David, reaching again.

David spun and ran.

"David!" Xander's footsteps slapped the stone floor behind him.

"I have to," David said, without slowing. "I can feel it. Maybe he's why we're here." He turned the corner and saw the lighted entrance to the torture chamber far ahead.

"David!"

David stopped and held his hands out to keep Xander from grabbing him. He said, "Shhh! Xander, please. We know where the portal is. We'll go right to it after . . ."

"After what?" Xander said. "After we're caught? Killed? There's nothing you can do for that guy."

"I have to *try*. Please. The torturer is just one guy. We've gotten away from much worse. The *Berserkers!*"

Xander's shoulders drooped. Even his faced drooped into a deep frown.

David said, "I'm supposed to do this. I know it. Like Jesse said."

"Did that knowledge come with a plan?"

David shook his head. "I'll . . . think of something . . ."

They stared at each other as seconds passed.

Finally Xander said, "This is stupid, maybe the stupidest thing you've ever done." He paused, probably hoping David would agree and change his mind. When he didn't, Xander said, "The first sign of danger, we run straight to the portal. Right?"

"The torturer's not going to just stand there," David said.

"Okay . . . okay . . ." Xander was thinking. "If it looks like we're in over our heads, like he's going to get us or something, *then* we run. Even if we haven't helped that guy. Deal?"

"Deal," David said. He liked that Xander had said *we*. He turned and walked toward the light.

Xander fell in beside him. "I can't believe we're doing this," he muttered quietly.

David swallowed. Neither could he.

The screaming grew louder with each step. At the chamber, David stepped in without pausing—if he hesitated, he knew he might not go through with it.

The torturer was leaning over the man on the rack. His hand was on the handle again.

"Stop it!" David yelled, walking toward him. "Stop it, now!"

"What are you *doing*?" Xander said behind him. "*That's* your plan?"

The torturer turned toward him. A momentary expression of surprise turned into amusement when he saw the child addressing him. Like David, he wore no shirt. He had on billowy black pants, cinched at the ankles, and sandals. Muscles rippled over his arms, shoulders, chest, and stomach. Long blond hair was pulled tightly over his scalp and bound into a ponytail. Blue eyes sparkled, and he flashed a charming smile at David.

In David's time, the guy would be modeling jeans or challenging Brad Pitt for the title of Heartthrob King. He was definitely not the hunchbacked, one-eyed ogre that the movies depicted, but David understood why modern people would think of torturers that way. Shouldn't evil things *look* evil? But he knew that wasn't the way things worked. If it were, Hitler could not have risen to power, because people would have seen right off how awful he was, and little kids wouldn't get into cars with strangers.

"Let him go!" David yelled. "Nobody deserves that! He's a *person!*"

The torturer stepped toward him. He opened his arms as if to say, *Now, what's all this about?* What he did say was, *"Sind Sie gekommen zu spielen, kleiner Junge?"*

David knew that his own words were as foreign to the man as the man's were to him. But he believed the torturer understood exactly what was on his mind. "How can you do this?" David said. "It's not right!"

As the man drew closer, David angled toward the back wall, trying to circle around the guy. He would not let the man come too close; someone like this probably knew a thousand ways to kill him with a touch.

The torturer shot a glance at Xander, directly behind David. The man reached behind his back. When his hand reappeared, it held a small dagger.

"David," Xander said. "That's it, man. Let's get out of here."

The man glared at David, obviously trying to figure out what they were up to. David wondered if the man thought he was dealing with a crazy kid and might get hurt. And *crazy* was exactly the way to describe his actions, he knew. If Xander wanted to put *him* on the rack, he couldn't blame him.

Xander shot around the table to stand beside him.

As if realizing the boys had put themselves in a position in which escape meant having to pass him again, the torturer grinned.

"Smooth move, Einstein," Xander said. "Now what?"

David turned to the wall behind him. Tools and devices—most of them for uses he thankfully didn't know—hung from pegs. He pulled down an axe. It was short with a triangular blade that appeared sinisterly sharp. He whipped it around.

The torturer's eyes opened wide. He darted toward the table, probably thinking he'd lean over it and jab David with the dagger.

David hefted the axe over his head, and the torturer stopped. He narrowed his eyes at the axe, then lowered them to David's face. David had a feeling the man was imagining all the terrible things he'd do to him once he had him subdued, chained, screaming like his other victims.

David slammed the axe down on the ropes holding the rack victim's wrists. The man's arms seemed to *unstretch*. He gasped. The torturer leaped forward, thrusting the dagger across the table. David jumped back.

Xander bumped past David, a big sword in both hands. He swung it at the torturer, who reeled away from the gleaming blade. "Go, David, run!" he said.

David shifted and brought the axe down on the ropes tied to the victim's legs. The injured man rolled off the table, thumping to the floor. He rose onto his hands and knees, crumpled, and rose again.

The torturer spat out a string of guttural words, fuming now that his "work" had been interrupted, his victim set free.

Xander shoved his shoulder into David. "If you don't move right now, I'm going to knock you out and *carry* you out of here!"

David cast a final glance at the man on the floor. He wanted to help him up, take him with them, but he knew that wasn't meant to be. Every second that passed, every thing they did to help the man, made the torturer angrier. If they pushed him too far, his fury would push away caution, driving him to attack harder. If he slipped past Xander's sword . . .

David couldn't even think about what would happen then.

"Let's go," he said.

Xander retraced their steps around the table, swinging the sword back and forth, back and forth at the torturer. The man looked like a vicious dog snapping at the end of its leash.

"Go behind me, David," Xander said. "Hurry!"

David did. He quick-stepped toward the passageway entrance. He resisted breaking into an all-out run, trying to let Xander sidestep in pace with him, keeping the torturer at bay.

The torturer moved with them. Every couple of steps, he stepped forward, swung the dagger, then jumped back as Xander responded with his own jab or swing.

David reached the passageway, reached out, and grabbed a handful of material at Xander's back. "We're at the passage!" he yelled. "Come on!" He tugged Xander out of the chamber.

Xander backpedaled as David pulled. David glanced back to see the torturer following them into the gloomy tunnel. The guy wasn't about to simply let these intruders waltz away.

Xander swung the sword. The blade clanged and sparked against the stone walls. The torturer could do nothing but pursue them, hoping Xander would trip or drop the sword or in some way present an opening that would be his last.

"Move, move!" Xander repeated. When they were almost at the intersecting corridor that led to the portal, he said, "I hope you're happy. All this guy's going to do is go back to work once we're gone. We didn't do anything to help!"

David said nothing. He didn't want to hear it. Maybe it hadn't worked out. Maybe it was just plain stupid. But how could you not breathe when your body needed oxygen? That's how *trying* to help that poor soul on the table had felt to him.

As they approached the side passageway, Xander said, "That's it. Go!"

David ran until he saw the cell with the shimmering back wall. He grabbed a bar and swung himself into the cell. A cold wind blew out of the portal, chilling his skin and making him pause.

Xander threw the sword at the torturer, stepped in, and shoved David through.

# thirty-nine

David fell onto a floor, which broke apart under his feet. Shards of pain jabbed into his eyes. He squinted against a harsh brightness: a sun that burned fiercely overhead *and* all around.

*Snow* . . . the whitest, most dazzling snow he had ever seen.

He crashed through an icy crust into flakes that were nothing like the fluffy stuff he'd skied on at Mammoth Mountain. This snow had seemed to crystallize into tiny Chinese throwing stars. He flipped and rolled, and an awful fact struck him as forcefully as the bitter cold—

*I'm not stopping!*

He somersaulted and tumbled down a steep incline, breaking a trench in the crust as he went. He clutched and clawed, but everything he touched slipped through his fingers or broke off in his hands. Scrambling, squirming, he pivoted, bringing his feet into a downhill inclination, and found himself skimming over the crust of icy snow on his butt.

Below him, at the base of the hill, the snow gave way to a narrow ledge of stone. Beyond that—nothing. A cliff. Far, far away, across an entire sky of empty air, huge mountain peaks pierced the clouds.

He screamed and rolled onto his bare stomach. The frosty crust chafed his skin like sandpaper. He clawed and scratched. Ice crystals splintered under his nails and shot away like sawdust. The toes of his sneakers streaked over the surface, as effective at gripping the ice as hockey pucks.

His descent made a sound like static in his ears. It occurred to him how silent death-by-falling would be. No explosions, no crunching metal or breaking glass. There would be wind, but certainly it would not be louder than your own pulsing heartbeat, so it didn't count.

*A sudden, unexpected death shouldn't be silent,* he thought. *It should be frantic and dramatic and noisy.*

Nothing like what happens in a fall. Maybe that's why people screamed on the way down.

Desperate, David pounded his cast into the snow's surface, gritting his teeth against the stabbing pain. His cast broke through, violently ripping through the crust like a bulldozer through a wall. His descent slowed . . . slowed . . . stopped.

Scrunching his eyes closed, he howled in pain. With his right hand he seized his left wrist and hugged it to his chest. He twisted around to see that he had stopped where the icy slope met the gray ledge of stone. Not twenty feet away, the world ended.

Xander's surprised shriek reached him. High up on the slope, his brother spun in circles, round and round, as he plunged down the hill.

A flash farther up the hill caught his eye. The torturer appeared to materialize against a shimmering ripple of air and drop to the snow. He began sliding, his eyes even wider than Xander's, which David would have thought impossible.

David scrambled up. Pain, like molten metal, shot up his arm. He fell onto his knees, screaming out again. Every pulse of blood his racing heart sent into his arm felt like a hammer blow.

He forced his eyes open to see Xander struggling to get his feet under him. His brother stood, his legs taking great strides down the hill, then plunged through the air, belly flopping on the crusty surface. Arms stretched out, skimming down on his stomach, he could have been Superman learning to fly—but he wasn't Superman and he couldn't fly, a fact that would become horrifically evident when he went over the cliff.

"Xander!" David screamed, pointing at the torturer skimming on the ice thirty feet behind his brother.

Hugging his arm, David stomped up the slope.

Xander was almost on him. His brother's hands skittered over the surface, doing nothing but kicking up snow crystals that flew back into his face.

David stomped, cracking the crust. Another stomp, and his right foot broke through. He did the same with his left foot. Wiggling, rocking, he dug himself in. He swung his injured arm out of harm's way, and Xander slammed into him like a tidal wave hitting a ship. Anchored in the snow, David bent backward.

Xander's arms crumpled. His head struck David and continued moving over David's chest and head. His body followed, sliding onto—over—David as though he were a ramp.

When David realized Xander wasn't stopping, he shot his right hand up and hooked his fingers into Xander's waistband. The force wrenched David's shoulder. He was yanked out of the hole, and together they slid toward the cliff.

But David's efforts had slowed his brother's momentum. When Xander hit the stone ledge, he came to a jittery stop. David coasted into him.

The sound of the torturer's descent—like the ripping of paper—increased rapidly as he approached.

"Roll!" Xander yelled "Roll!"

David felt Xander twisting away, and he rolled with him.

The torturer's hand slapped at David's arm and shoulder as he sailed past. David craned his head to watch the man hit the rocky ledge, slide, roll, and disappear over the edge: "Aaaaaaaaaaaaaahhh . . ."

Then nothing. The sound of the sky breathing over the boys.

David squeezed his eyelids together, feeling tears push against them. He was lying on his back, too aware of his body to care about anything else. Bolts of pain shot out of his right shoulder into his neck. His left arm formed a V on the ground beside him, like the wing of a dead bird. It blazed in agony. His fist was still locked onto Xander's pants. His teeth gnashed together.

"Holy cow," Xander said, panting. "David? You okay?" He nudged David's hand, then gently pried David's fingers open. He crawled to him and cupped a palm over David's cheek. "You saved me, Dae. You did it. I would have gone over the edge like that guy, if you hadn't stopped me. Dae?"

David could not stop crying. He *hurt*. His broken arm . . . his shoulder . . . his abraded chest and stomach . . . his legs and back . . . He cried from the pain, and he didn't want to stop, because it eased the agony a little bit. His chest hitched in jerky motions as he took small gulps of air to fuel his sobs.

"Oh, David," Xander said. He carefully moved David's arms for him, crossing them over his chest. David felt a warmth envelope him and knew Xander had covered him with the Union army coat. Xander pushed the two front halves under him on either side.

"How are your legs?" Xander said. He brushed the snow off David's jeans.

David felt his sneakers come off and heard Xander knocking the snow out of them. His brother slipped them back on and tied them tight.

David dialed down the tears. His breathing remained in choppy crying mode, but it was getting smoother.

Xander's footsteps crunched over the snow and stopped after a few paces. He said, "We gotta get out of here—fast, before we freeze to death."

"Where . . ." David's voice was barely audible to his own ears, let alone Xander's. He tried again: "Where are we?"

Xander's feet crunched back to David's side. "No clue."

David blinked and found his eyeballs drowning in tears. He slipped a hand out from under the coat and wiped them. His temples and ears were soaked . . . and *cold*. The wetness had begun to ice up.

Xander stood over him, looking out beyond the cliff. He was hugging himself, furiously rubbing his hands over his biceps. He wore a short-sleeved button-up shirt. His lips were turning blue. Through chattering teeth, he said, "Well, at least it's beautiful." Plumes of vapor came out with each word.

David coughed out a pathetic laugh. "Yeah, the same way a great white shark is before it eats you."

"Guess we took care of that torturer guy, huh? Man! Bet he was surprised."

David tried to laugh again, but he hurt too much.

Xander crunched beside him. "So?" he said. "Are you dizzy? Any mixed-up memories?"

David squinted at him, uncomprehending.

"You know," Xander said. "Did cutting that guy from the rack . . . getting rid of the torturer . . . did it change history? Can you tell?"

David closed his eyes again and shook his head. "Nothing like what happened back at the Civil War." He breathed. "Maybe we didn't save him after all." He started to cry again. "Maybe we didn't do anything but almost get killed."

He wanted to cry again. It wasn't just the feeling that he'd failed or the pain or being tired . . . it was *everything*.

"Maybe you just can't tell what changed," Xander said. "Could be not everything we do is noticeable. We made a difference, but it's too subtle for us to know about it."

David draped his arm over his face, across his eyes. "I'm sorry," he said. "I shouldn't have done that. I shouldn't have tried."

Xander nudged him. "Don't say that. Like Toria said, you feel bad when people on *TV* get hurt." He paused. "Follow your heart, Dae, but try to keep it beating, okay? If you want to do it, you can help a lot of people using the portals. But you can't if you're dead."

"You really think we can do that—help people in the other worlds?"

"*While* we're looking for Mom." Xander considered his words, then added, "But not that way. Not stupid."

David nodded.

Xander tapped his arm. "How are you feeling?"

David moaned. "Let me think about it." And he did: his skin was warming up, a little; the sledgehammer-pounding in his broken arm had subsided into a throb; and the throbbing in his shoulder had settled into a dull ache. He said, "Better."

Xander grabbed his shoulders to help him up. "Then we better go."

"Where?"

"Is the coat . . ." Xander looked at it with hope. "Is it pulling yet?"

David held it up between them. It hung limp. "No," he said. "You think it's going to?"

"It got us out of the torture chamber," Xander said. "We just have to not freeze to death while we're waiting for it." He looked up the slope. The hill stopped just above the place where they came into this world—marked by the broken crust

at the top of their slide-tracks. Beyond, the mountain continued its jaggy, rocky ascent into the sky. "I think there's some
kind of flat area up there," he said. "Maybe a pass or a road.
That's the place to start."

He stepped off the gray stone ledge onto the snow.

"Xander," David said. He extended the coat to him.

Xander scowled at it. "Are you kidding?" he said. "Put it
on."

"You s-s-sure?" David's entire body trembled from the
cold.

"Don't be dumb," Xander said.

David slipped his right arm in, hissing in pain as he did.
He draped the left side over his broken arm. Xander crouched
in front of him to button it up.

"Thanks for not being mad at me," David said.

"Who said I'm not mad?" Xander said, not taking his eyes
off the buttons. His hands were shaking so much, each button
took ten seconds. He smiled up at David. "Don't worry about
it. We're still figuring all this out." He finished and tugged the
coat down. It was too big, hanging almost to David's knees.

"You were something back there," David said, forcing a
smile. "Swinging that sword. Man, you saved us."

Xander shrugged. "We watch out for each other. That's
what we do." He stood, said, "Here, I should have thought of
this before . . ." He unbuckled his belt and took it off.

"What?" David said.

"A sling," Xander said, "for your arm." He buckled the belt and slipped it over David's head.

David tucked it inside the coat and rested his arm in the loop.

"Better?" Xander said.

"Yeah. Thanks." He tried to smile, but his lips trembled too much. He said, "What if we're too deep in the worlds for the coat to work?"

Xander smiled. "Then I hope we like this place." He started up the hill.

# CHAPTER

## forty

They trudged up the slope, gaining traction from the gouges and depressions they had made on their way down. The final thirty feet were more treacherous. Several times one or the other of them slipped back to the holes they'd first made plunging into this world. They finally figured out that pounding their feet through the icy crust before taking a step did the trick. It was a slow, grueling climb.

At the top, David collapsed onto his back, panting. He

chugged out puffs of smoky vapor, like an idling steam train.

Xander stood, then bent over to catch his breath. "Come on, man," he said. "We gotta keep moving." When David didn't move, Xander grabbed his collar to tug him up. "I mean it."

David rolled over and pushed himself up, groaning like an old man. He looked down the length of slope to the cliff. "I can't believe what a close call that was," he said.

"It won't matter that we didn't go over," Xander said, "if we don't find shelter soon."

"Shelter?" David said, in a voice more whiny than he'd intended.

"Shelter first," Xander said, "*then* the portal home."

They were standing on a path about twenty feet wide, the slope on one side, a steep rock cliff on the other. It followed the contours of the mountain, rising and falling, swooping left, then right. One direction sloped gradually upward. The opposite way headed down.

Xander pointed at the ground. "Look." The snow had been beaten down by the passage of what seemed to be wagons, vehicles, animals, people.

"That's a good sign," Xander said.

"If they're friendly," David added.

"Hey, if there's people, there's gotta be a place to warm up." Xander faced the upward direction. After a distance, the path curved left and out of sight. He turned the other way, where a longer stretch of path showed itself. Eventually, it bent right and disappeared. Beyond the bend, only sky.

Xander pointed back in the other direction. "I'm thinking up. Just a feeling."

"Xander," David said, shaking uncontrollably.

"What?" Xander said, impatient and obviously baffled by the smile David had forced onto his face.

"It's the other way." David gestured with his head.

"What is?"

"The portal."

"How do you—" Xander's eyes dropped to the bottom hem of the coat. It was fluttering, one side billowing out away from David's left leg, the other pressed tightly against his right. "Yeah! I knew we could count on it."

David laughed—despite the cold and all his aches and pains, he laughed, releasing big clouds into the air.

"Let's go!" Xander said. He gave David a little shove, and they started down the path.

It didn't take long for the cold to cut through their excitement. They shuffled along, pulling their shoulders, arms, and heads as near their bodies as possible.

"Xander," David said. His teeth chattered.

"Hmmm?"

"How do you think there were *two* portals?" He realized they could discuss it another time, maybe slumped on the family's cozy sofa, wrapped in blankets, holding steaming mugs of hot chocolate. But he needed a distraction from the cold. Anything would do, and this was what was on his mind.

Xander shuffled on and said, "Probably there always have been. We just never knew about them because we've relied on the antechamber items to show us the right one. Could be, an open portal automatically opens another."

*Whoa*, David thought. That was something that had never occurred to him. It meant that you could end up *anywhere*, not just the world the house showed you.

"What if . . ." Xander said and stopped.

"What?"

"Did you hear something?"

They stared at each other for a time, listening, freezing. David shook his head, and they continued on.

"What if," Xander said, "getting the doctor for that guy and rescuing Nana were two *separate* things we were supposed to do?"

David shuffled, shuffled. His breath kept pluming out in front of him, and he kept walking into it. He said, "So, the two things just *happened* to occur at the same place and almost the same time, using the same antechamber items?" He shook his head, skeptical.

"Maybe it was a coincidence, maybe not,'" Xander said. "What if our messing around there the first time *triggered* the other one. Looking for Mom—drawing Bob—kind of, I don't know, kind of put Nana on the front burner."

One of Mom's expressions. David knew it meant making something a priority, something that had to be done right away.

When David didn't reply, Xander said, "I don't know, Dae. It's something to figure out. Move faster."

CHAPTER

# forty-one

The coat billowed in front of David, making him look barrel-chested and fat.

As they approached the bend, Xander said, "Dae, it's not pulling *too* hard, is it?"

David glanced at him, saw true concern. "Not yet. Why?"

Xander stuck his arm out, stopping him. "Maybe you should take it off."

"What? It's freezing."

"Would you rather be cold . . . or hurled off a cliff?" He nodded toward the end of the visible path.

David hurried to unbutton himself. "Think it would do that?"

"I don't know," Xander said, "but why find out the hard way? The pull *does* get strong."

Xander slipped the coat off him. "Oh, Dae," he said.

David followed his brother's gaze to his chest and stomach. His torso was so red it looked like someone had beat him with a paddle. There were a million pinpricks of blood, like a really bad rash. "It's from sliding down the slope," he said. Looking at the damage to his skin, his breathing picked up. He swallowed, sorry for himself.

"Holy cow!" Xander said, gaping at David's stomach.

"What?" said David, thinking: gushing blood, bruises, a shard of something jabbed into him that he couldn't feel because of the cold.

Xander flashed a grin. "You're getting a six-pack, dude."

David smiled. "I wish." As ornery as his brother could be, he sure knew how to pick up his spirits when he wanted to. "It doesn't hurt as bad as it looks. Just a little." He shivered.

Xander said, "Let's do this." He draped the coat over David's shoulders. "Hold it closed from the inside. Better?"

David nodded.

"Just let it go if it heads someplace bad."

"Don't worry."

About twenty paces before the path curved around a steep outcropping of stone, David felt the coat starting to nudge him that way. He took that as a sign the coat—or any of the antechamber items—wasn't going to lead them where they couldn't go.

Xander stepped close to the edge of the path and peered over. "Oh, man. It's straight down. No slope at all. I mean, I can't even see the bottom." He backed away.

Around the bend, the path wove gently back and forth, giving them a long view of it, maybe a half mile. It sloped down shallowly, then went up a hill and disappeared.

"How's the pull?" Xander said.

"Getting stronger."

"Let's move faster," Xander said again, rubbing his arms.

They started jogging. After a minute, Xander stopped. He crouched and pulled David down. He pointed to something up on the mountain above them, just ahead. It was a man, dressed completely in fur. His boots might have been leather, it was hard to tell at that distance. A tight-fitting fur cap covered the top of his head. Long black hair spilled out from under the cap and whipped around in the wind. He was facing away from the boys, and David could make out a quiver of arrows strapped diagonally across his back. His left hand held a bow.

As they watched, another man appeared beside him. This one was similarly dressed, but carried a sword. A third man stepped into view. All three angled their attention beyond the hill at the far end of this current stretch of path. As quickly as they had appeared, they vanished.

"Who are they?" David whispered.

Xander shook his head. He looked ahead, then over his shoulder. Indecision etched old-man lines in his face.

"We have to keep going," David said. The tug of the coat, urging him to continue along the path, was getting difficult to reign in. Even if they wanted to turn back, he doubted the coat would let them.

Xander stood and pulled David to the inside edge of the path, where the stone formed slanted walls. "Single file," he whispered. "Stay close to the mountain."

They continued toward the hill. Despite continually checking, neither of them saw the men again.

As they started climbing the hill, David touched Xander's arm. He pointed at the coat. Below the spot where his hand held the front together, the material stood straight out, as though David had strapped a blue, cloth-covered table to his belly. It vibrated with tension.

Xander smiled. "Close," he said. "Right over the hill, I bet."

The ground shook, a quick rumble, then nothing. Xander's eyes widened. "Did you feel—" It shook again, again, again.

A rumbling sound reached them, the low tremble of drums. The tremors under their feet continued.

Xander grabbed David's shoulder. "What does that remind you of?"

"An earthquake?" David didn't want to be on a mountain during an earthquake. Who knew what would come tumbling down on them.

"*Jurassic Park*," Xander said. "When the T. Rex is coming and the coffee starts trembling."

"You think we're in *dinosaur* times?" David almost screamed.

"I'm not saying that," Xander said. "But *something's* coming."

"We have to get to the portal!" David said. "Now!" He ducked out of Xander's grasp and ran up the hill. He half expected Xander to grab him or at least call his name. Instead, his brother caught up, ran alongside. Both of them scanned the rocks above them. Nothing.

They hit the top of the hill, and David grabbed Xander's arm. A cloud of vapors billowed from his mouth, giving form to his silent scream.

CHAPTER

# forty-two

An elephant charged up the other side at the boys.

A *war* elephant: Armor covered its head. Its tusks curved forward from the sides of its mouth—impossibly large swords. Behind its head sat a man wearing red, flowing robes. He held a short rod, which he used to tap the animal's head. A harness crossed over his chest and held him to the front of an ornate wooden box, which bounced precariously on the elephant's back.

Three men—obviously soldiers—stood in the box. They wore metal helmets and breastplates. Two gripped bows and arrows, ready for a fight. The third brandished a polelike spear—a pike, long enough to impale people on the ground.

Behind this lead animal, a dozen more trotted, all with drivers and soldiers on their backs. Men on horseback rode among the larger animals. They galloped alongside, some crossing in front, some in full stride heading for the front. Farther back, foot soldiers marched, carrying a forest of pikes and shields that sparkled like the scales of a dragon. Behind them, more elephants and cavalrymen.

The army completely filled the passage as far as David could see. In the distance, the path curved out of sight, the army curving with it.

David started to spin around, planning to run—up the mountain, back the way they had come, anywhere. Xander shoved him from behind, toward the elephant. As he fell, he craned around to see Xander on the side of the path. Terror twisted his face into a very un-Xanderlike mask. David realized his brother had not shoved him: it had been the *coat!* It wanted to go home.

David slid down the hill on his back. He batted the coat flaps off his chest, but he was *lying* on it—and it was moving. The coat carried him like a magic carpet into the elephant's path.

Xander yelled, "Roll off!"

David kicked the ground and spun, but it was too late. The animal was nearly on top of him. The thing reared up on its hind legs. Its front feet pedaled in the air. It didn't trumpet as much as it *screamed*, a hissing, canyon-deep bellow that announced its displeasure at this strange creature slithering toward it.

The beast's foot came down on David's legs—or would have had David not thrown his legs up at the last moment. He bumped into its leg, and it reared up again. He slid under it—not fast enough. The pizza-sized foot dropped, aiming for his head. He rolled, and the foot stomped the coat. David lay facedown on top of the coat's front panel. He rolled again, slipping his arm free from Xander's makeshift sling. He pushed up onto his hands and knees.

A third time, the elephant reared. The coat began sliding away. David grabbed it. More than anything, he did not want to lose it.

The coat whipped like a flag in his hand. He stood, backed away from the animal.

Its heavy tusks swung toward David's head like ivory baseball bats. He ducked. The tusks passed over him, then swung back. The beast stepped toward the cliff.

"David!" Xander yelled.

While his name still rang in his ears, something grabbed his left arm and shoved it. His arm slammed into the ground, bringing him down with it. He gaped at a pike pinning the bandage-covered cast to the ground. His eyes followed it to the soldier standing in the box on the elephant's back.

He held the pike in both hands, his face twisted with cruel intentions. He yelled, *"Nativi! Prepari morire!"* and pulled back on the pike.

David's arm went with it. He rose off the ground and landed on his feet, his arm raised and crossing in front of his face. But the spearhead of the pike, which had pierced his cast without hitting his arm, now hovered three inches in front of his eye. He jerked his head sideways as the soldier thrust the pike. The spearhead nicked David's ear. It carried his arm with it, and the cast cracked against his head.

The soldier pulled back, ripping the pike from the cast.

Xander came screaming down the hill. An archer in the elephant box raised his bow, taking aim.

The soldier with the pike did not avert his eyes from David. The spearhead wavered like a shaky hand three feet from David's chest.

An arrow thunked into the neck of the archer who had taken aim at Xander. He gurgled out a scream and fell backward out of David's line of sight—until he thumped to the ground on the other side of the elephant.

Two more arrows struck the soldier with the pike: one in the shoulder, one in the neck. The man dropped the pike. The spearhead bit into the ground between David's feet. The soldier pitched forward. He tumbled out of the box, rolled over the animal's rear end, and crashed to the ground.

The last soldier in the box shot an arrow. It sailed high, toward the rocks above the pass. David followed it with his eyes. The cliff above the road was lined with the fur-covered men he and Xander had seen earlier. One of them shot an arrow, and David followed it back to the soldier on the elephant. It struck his breastplate and zinged away. The soldier flinched, reversed a step, and sent his own arrow flying.

Xander stomped up to David. He grabbed him and yanked him back toward the wall under the furry warriors.

CHAPTER

# forty-three

David plopped down against the mountain. The road here was narrow, and even with his back pressed into the stone, David found the elephant too close for his liking.

A shadow flashed over him, coming from the mountain. One of the furry men landed on the elephant's back. He clung to the outside of the box. The soldier lunged at him, wielding an arrow like a dagger. Fur Man dodged it, raised a short sword, and chopped.

His body shielded David from seeing where the blow landed. But that it did was clear: a scream filled the air, and the soldier fell off the far side of the elephant. He did not thump to the ground as the others had done. He simply vanished over the cliff.

The beast—sensing or seeing how near it was to the edge—turned from it. Its tusks swung toward the boys.

David pulled his feet in and leaned into the wall behind him, wishing he could somehow climb *into* the stone.

The path was not wide enough for that huge animal to turn around, but it was turning anyway. The driver furiously beat the rod against the animal's head. He yelled commands in a foreign language. One of the elephant's tusks struck the rock cliff and scraped against it.

Fur Man was in the box now, directly behind the driver. He raised the sword over his head with both hands.

The elephant stepped back. Its hind foot stomped down on the crest of the cliff. The ground under it crumbled. Its leg went over. The rear half of its massive body collapsed, sending a shockwave into the ground that David felt. The animal's other rear leg kicked, pushing its rear over the edge. Its front legs pressed into the ground, but it could not stop its backward slide. Its feet left deep gouges in the earth. Lifting its head, raising its tusks like outstretched arms, it let loose with that deep, hissing bellow.

Fur Man sprang up from behind its head. He planted a foot

on the plate between the animal's eyes, and leaped between its tusks.

The beast went over.

Fur Man landed on his feet, directly in front of David and Xander. He had a straight nose, high cheekbones, a short-cropped beard, and intelligent green eyes. David thought that in any other setting he could have been a nobleman. Glaring at David and Xander, the man cocked his sword high above his head.

David let out a squeaky yelp—he couldn't help it—and threw his hands up. He watched the man through splayed fingers: he would close his eyes when the blow came, but closing them now and *waiting* seemed much worse.

"Wait, wait, wait!" Xander yelled. "Please."

The man turned his head to squint at Xander from the corner of his eye.

To David, the look said, *Can I trust you, boy?* and he allowed himself a sliver of hope. He whispered, "Please."

The man nodded once, then he ran down the hill toward the army. He passed an elephant trotting the other direction, no driver, no soldiers. The ground trembled as the creature tromped past the boys, crested the hill, and disappeared.

David saw that other men dressed in fur, hundreds of them, had already engaged the army. Many of them were perched on ledges above the path, picking soldiers off with arrows. Some,

like Fur Man, had descended to fight on foot. They were slicing at the horsemen, pulling them off their steeds. The neat,
even ranks of infantrymen had morphed into roving bands of
fighters. Hundreds were trying to climb the steep mountain
walls to get at their attackers; others went after the fur men
who'd come among them.

"David," Xander said, "I think I know who they are. Those
soldiers."

"Hannibal's army," David said, straining his arms to reel in
the coat. It flapped and snapped, becoming as stiff as a board
for seconds at a time. "Carthaginians."

"That would put us in the Alps," Xander said. "200 B.C.
Something like that."

"That's a *long* way from home," David said, feeling every
word.

The coat snapped straight and lunged forward, toward the
chaos of battle. Trying to hang on, David flipped onto his
stomach. The coat didn't stop. It flapped and lunged, like a
sled dog pulling a heavy load.

"Hey," Xander said behind him. "Stop!"

"I can't!"

"Let go of it!" Xander's feet pounded behind him.

"No way!" David said. Losing the coat would leave them
stranded. He could not imagine finding a portal without an
antechamber item leading them to it.

Xander grabbed one of David's ankles, then the other.

David used the leverage to pull the coat to him. He found an armhole and pushed into it.

"What are you doing?" Xander said.

"If it's taking off," David said, "then I'm taking off with it. Don't let go." He found the other armhole and worked his cast inside. The cast had crumbled and shrunk since it was new, allowing a snug fit. He rolled onto his back.

The coat slid up over his head. It lunged, pulling David a few feet. Xander stumbled with him.

"Help me," David said.

Xander got on his knees and walked his hands up David's legs. He sat on David's shins, tugged the coat down, and started buttoning it up. "You know, I did a paper about war elephants for history a couple years ago," Xander said. "Never thought I'd see one."

"Anything we can use?" That's all David wanted to know.

Xander shook his head. "They would charge an enemy line, trampling and clobbering them with their tusks. And their height gave the Carthaginians riding them a great angle of attack."

"Tell me something I don't know."

Xander worked a button in and moved to the top one. "Those boxes on their backs? I think they're called *howdahs*."

David frowned. "We're not playing a trivia game here," he said. "Anything *useful*?"

"Like what, go for their eyes?"

"Really?"

"No, not really," Xander said. "We're not fighting them. We're *evading* them."

"Tell me this, anyway," David said. "Who are those guys they're fighting?"

"Gauls, maybe," Xander said. "Or one of the native tribes up here. There were a lot of them."

*"Fur men,"* David said. "Are you done?"

Xander patted David's chest. He looked up at the battle ahead of them. "You sure about this?"

David made a firm face. He said, "Strong and courageous."

Xander repeated it, then let a long breath out his nose. The vapors streamed out like smoke.

"Help me up," David said. When they were standing, hugging each other to keep David from sailing away, David said, "Hold on to the collar."

Xander turned him around to face their course. The battle raged along a mile of cliffside path. Elephants reared, stomping down on men and horses. Arrows flew back and forth. Swords and shields glinted. The cacophony of screams, yells, bellows, and clanging weapons was enough to send the bravest warrior running for home.

"Let's do it," David said.

# forty-four

With Xander gripping the back of his collar, David ran into the battle the way only a crazy person would: at full speed. The coat, billowing in front, pulled him along. If he wasn't running faster than he ever had, then he was at least running *as* fast, and doing it with much less effort. The effort came in keeping his feet under him, in not letting the coat outpace him and cause him to fall.

The first combatants were thirty yards away: a Carthaginian

with a pike and a fur man with a sword. The Carthaginian lunged, the fur man parried. David angled close to the stone cliffs. As he passed, the fur man's sword sliced off the head of the pike. The Carthaginian dropped the weapon and reached for his own sword as the fur man rushed in. David fought the urge to look.

Ahead, an elephant panicked. It reared up and pawed at a fur man waving a sword at it. The animal swung its head. Its tusks brought down a galloping horse, whose rider flipped over its head. The cavalryman landed at the feet of the fur man, who plunged his sword in.

"Ohhh," David moaned. He didn't want to see this. He wished he could close his eyes and trust the coat to guide him safely through the carnage: the time-traveling version of auto-pilot. But he'd seen how the items blew back to the portals, bouncing off trees, tearing through bushes . . . like trash caught in a wind. If he weren't steering the coat, he was sure it would careen into elephants, horses, people.

Not that he did much better. As he moved into the heavi-est concentration of combatants, he began bumping into Carthaginians and fur men alike, shoving them out of the way, tripping over them. His soccer feet came in handy, and he tried to warn Xander: "Jump!" "Left!" "Duck!"

He came upon a narrow section of path, packed with fighters. On the right, next to the mountain, two men clashed swords. On the left, near the cliff edge, a Carthaginian on horseback was leaning low, swinging a sword at a fur man and trying to get the horse to tromp the man. And dead center were two men in weaponless hand-to-hand combat.

David headed for them.

The Carthaginian punched his opponent, who dropped to one knee. The Carthaginian saw David coming. The guy girded himself, leaning forward to take whatever it was this kid was dishing out.

David plowed into him with his right shoulder. The Carthaginian went down with an "Ooooph!" and David leaped over him.

"Yeah!" he started to say, but—

Xander stumbled over the man and yanked down on David's collar.

"Yeeeeeee!" David screamed. His feet flew up, his head fell back. He landed flat on his back, unintentionally mimicking the Carthaginian he had decked: "Oooph!"

Xander's fist dug into the top of David's spine. The coat dragged him two feet before Xander's grip stopped him.

David twisted to look back. The soldier had hold of Xander's foot. The man bared his teeth and growled. Xander kicked at him.

"Xander!" David yelled.

Xander kicked. "I'm working on it."

An arrow thunked into the ground next to Xander's shoulder.

David saw the shooter, a Carthaginian in a *howdah* twenty yards away. The elephant he rode was sweeping its tusks at three fur men. They poked at it with swords, apparently trying to drive it over the edge. The archer nocked another arrow.

"Xander!" he said. "Roll away!"

The fur man the soldier on the ground had been fighting returned, fists pounding. The soldier let go of Xander. An arrow struck the fur man's chest.

Xander shook his head, wiped at his face. Blood was splattered across his cheek. He rose, lifting David. "Go!" he said.

David ran—straight into the side of a horse. The horseman glared down at him and raised his sword. Instinctively, David threw up his hands to protect himself.

*Stupid!* The sword would slice through his hands and arms and thunk into his skull. *Drop!* he told himself. *Go under the horse!*

But, lightning fast, the horseman grabbed David's wrist.

Xander tugged at David's collar, trying to pull him free. The horseman held firm, a mean little smile on his lips.

Xander came around, tried to reach for the hand, but it was too high. He yelled and punched the horse. The horseman kicked him in the jaw, and Xander flew away, letting go of the collar.

The horseman lifted David straight up. When they were face-to-face, he hauled back on the sword again. He had a clear angle on David's head or neck or just about any part of him.

The coat lunged, sending David crashing into the horseman. David caught a glimpse of the man's shocked expression before they both tumbled off the horse. David hit the ground and rolled away, assisted by the coat's pull. By the time he hopped up, he was twenty feet away from the man, who twisted and sliced his sword into the ground. He scowled at the nothing he had killed.

David backed against the mountain's stone wall. The coat pulled him backward along it. He grabbed a small outcropping and stopped. "Xander!" he called.

The horseman spotted David, and his mouth dropped open. An arrow pierced the ground by the man's outstretched arm. From its angle, David guessed it had come from high on the mountain. Another arrow nicked the man's shoulder. He scrambled under his horse.

Xander darted around it, rubbing his jaw. He ran to David and grabbed his collar. "Try not to run into anything else," he said.

# forty-five

David stayed close to the wall. Most of the fighting was in the middle or outer edge of the path, where the Carthaginians could aim at the fur men on the mountain, and it was here the fur men landed when they jumped down to fight. It was easy going, until he noticed a group of Carthaginians aligned beside the mountain. They were jabbing pikes at fur men on a ledge above them.

The first Carthaginian saw them coming. He leveled his

pike at David. When David angled out to skirt the men, the Carthaginian moved with him.

*What's with that?* David thought. Just mean-spiritedness? Orders to kill everyone? Or was it the sense people had that time travelers didn't belong there, an intuition bothering them?

Didn't matter. They had to handle it. David returned to the mountain wall, drawing the Carthaginian there too.

"Let go," he told Xander.

"What?"

"Do it!" he said. "I'll meet you on the other side."

Xander released his grip. "Other side of what?"

David moved faster. The coat was barreling to the portal now. He hoped it would maintain its momentum. He ran straight for the pike. Its spearhead glinted in the sun.

*Don't go too soon*, he thought. *Or too late!*

He hoped the coat would let him guide it—as it had when he rolled away from the horseman, which inspired his current plan.

The Carthaginian, brow furrowed, realized David wasn't stopping. He braced himself for the jolt of David's chest hitting his weapon.

When David was so close he could see a chip in the spearhead, he dived under it. The coat carried him forward. He tucked his arms in, turned his body, and rolled. He crashed into the legs of the Carthaginian. The man went down behind him.

David had planned on continuing to roll, just bowling down everyone in his path. But the first impact spun him ninety degrees, and he hit the next Carthaginian with his feet. The guy landed on David's back and tumbled off. David pushed at the ground and rotated. His hip caught the following Carthaginian.

David went down the line like that, sliding, rolling, spinning. He took down ten pike-poking men, by his count.

Then he angled closer to the wall and began grabbing at stones to stop himself. His hands kept slipping off as the coat dragged him backward along the ground. His attempts to brake did slow the coat down; Xander was catching up. He was directly behind David now, displaying a huge open-mouthed grin.

He called, "That was the coolest thing I've ever seen!"

Behind Xander, a Carthaginian got to his feet. He picked up a pike and threw it at Xander.

"Look out!" David said.

Xander ducked and looked back. But the pike was not designed for throwing. Its heavy spearhead immediately dived into the ground.

David seized a vertical ledge and jerked to a stop. The coat continued to tug at him.

Xander reached him, kneeling to grab his arms.

The Carthaginian behind them picked up the pike again— way back, but David thought the guy's pride or nastiness might drive him to pursue them. "Get me up," David said. "We gotta go."

Another hundred yards of running and dodging. They started past a small, snow-covered meadow that opened up on the mountain side of the path. It was surrounded by cliffs, giving it the appearance of an amphitheater. A congregation of tall gray boulders, like boxcars standing on end, occupied the area farthest from the path.

The coat pulled David into this meadow, directing him to the boulders.

"Xander! It's here!"

"Yes!"

Hoofbeats echoed against the stone cliffs. David glanced back. The Carthaginian David had knocked off the horse was charging toward them! Sword in hand, he urged his steed into a gallop.

"Go, Dae! Go!"

David was already running all out through the snow. Any quicker and he'd lose control and fall.

The horseman was gaining.

"We're not going to make it," Xander said.

The beating of the horse's hooves grew louder, louder.

"David!"

David looked. The horseman was pulling beside them. He leaned out, taking swings at Xander. The boulders were twenty seconds away. The Carthaginian leaped for Xander.

But he hadn't leaped. He landed in the snow, an arrow jutting from his back.

"David, look."

Standing at the edge of the border between path and meadow was Fur Man, the one David thought looked like a nobleman. He already had another arrow nocked on his bow, ready to make it fly. The man nodded at the boys. Xander raised his hand.

The coat pulled David around a boulder. His shoulder smacked it hard.

*Of course.*

Behind the boulder, the portal shimmered, and for a moment David forgot about his aches and pains.

He jumped, Xander right on his back.

CHAPTER

# forty-six

David went through as though he'd plunged off a waterfall, arms spinning, feet kicking. He landed on his toes, crashed to his knees, then did a perfect face-plant. He rolled away just as Xander's feet hit the floor. His brother kept moving, slammed headlong into a door, and fell back on his rump.

The door behind them slammed.

*The door! The portal door!*

David sat up. His head jerked around like a chicken's as he took in the room: bench, hooks, two doors.

"Xander!" he said. "We're back! We're home!" He laughed.

Xander *whooped*. He high-fived David, who bent and kissed the floor over and over.

The Harper's Ferry rifle was where it always was when they found this particular antechamber, on the bench, leaning against the wall. The other items they had brought into the Civil War world were hanging on hooks: the two kepis and the gray Confederate coat.

David pushed himself off the floor, moaning and groaning, feeling well beyond his years. He struggled out of the Union army coat and hung it next to the other. "There ya go," he said, as if comforting a puppy. "Back where you belong. Thanks for getting us home."

A wind blew in from under the portal door.

David sighed, sat on the bench. When the boys returned to their own world, the wind always came for the things that belonged in the one they'd just left, from weapons to the smallest particles. "Guess it's going to be doing triple duty this time," he said.

It billowed around the room, whisking over the boys, through their clothes and hair. Then it swished under the door, a million bits of dirt and whatever else it had found tapping against the wood floor and door like the patter of rain on a window. David felt a tingling over his ribs. He looked down to see the dried blood Xander had smeared there breaking up and flying away. He rubbed the spot. "It took the blood."

Xander rubbed his cheek. "Off of me too? That fur man's blood?"

David nodded.

"Well," Xander said, "the guy did die twenty-two hundred years ago."

David looked at his chest, abraded from the slide down the icy slope. The redness had faded slightly, but it still appeared as though Chuck Norris had used him as a punching bag.

"You might need to see a doctor about that," Xander said.

"Oh, this'll just make the day of that doctor who accused Dad of breaking my arm." He gently poked his chest. "I think this'll be all right, but I don't know about my arm." He barely lifted it off his thigh and grimaced in pain. "I think I re-broke it."

"I'll check with Dad," Xander said, standing. "Get you some painkillers."

David closed his eyes and leaned back against the wall. "All I want right now is a long, hot bath." He laughed quietly.

"What?"

"'Member that scene in *Raiders of the Lost Ark*," David said, "where Indiana Jones is pointing to all the places on his body that hurt?"

"And Marion kissed them," Xander said.

David groaned. "Well, I got Indy beat in the banged-up department."

"And I'm not going to kiss you," Xander said. "I like the scene in *Jaws* better, where Quint and Hooper are comparing scars."

"We can definitely do that!"

"You know," Xander said, his voice growing serious. "After all that, we didn't do what we came home from school to do."

David instantly knew: "Young Jesse. Xander, we promised."

Xander frowned. "We'll get back there, Dae. We tried."

"No matter how much we do, there's always more."

"At least that one, going back to see Jesse and the house being built, isn't so dangerous," Xander said.

"I *want* to go there," David agreed.

Xander gave David a hand off the bench. David said, "How long have we been gone?"

"Maybe hours," Xander said. "I don't care what Keal or Dad or anyone says, I'm not going back to school today."

After all they'd gone through, going to school seemed . . . ridiculous times ten. Dad was firm about keeping up appearances—such as going to school—so they could stay in the house and keep looking for Mom. But for crying out loud! If Dad knew half of the stuff they'd gone through, he'd tell them to stay home for the rest of the year.

"You know," Xander said, "Dad might not have a problem with our staying home if you write that paper like you said."

"What paper?"

"About how we changed the Civil War. All those things you said back in the woods."

David rubbed his lips, thinking.

"How Grant died in 1862?" Xander prompted. "And that caused the war to last a lot longer? How two million people died before we changed history, instead of six hundred thousand?"

"Oh, man," David said, frustrated and more than a little confused. "I remember saying those things, but I can't remember why."

"Jesse was right," Xander said. "After history changes, he—I guess you too, now—remembers the *old* history for a while, but it fades fast. That's why he always tried to write it down."

David was mad at himself. "I didn't get a chance!" he said. "We went right into those other worlds."

Xander put his hand on David's shoulder. "I'm not *blaming* you," he said. "Do it next time."

"Hey," David said, brightening. "We can have a little kit ready. You know, paper, pens, a tape recorder."

"Just make sure you come back home after a change," Xander said, smiling. "Stop your reckless world-hopping ways." He opened the door and held it for David.

David stepped through and stopped. The hallway could not have been more damaged if a bull had rampaged through it. The top of an accent table was propped against the wall, the legs broken off and scattered on the floor; wall lights were twisted off-kilter, one had been knocked to the floor; a strip of molding from around a door had been ripped away—it jutted out of the wall like a spear. Across the hall from him, someone had hit the wall hard: the indentation was the size and shape of a human head.

Xander pushed past him. "*Holy*—Keal!" He ran toward the landing. On the floor, Keal lay sprawled facedown.

CHAPTER

# forty-seven

FRIDAY, 10:47 A.M.

David's stomach lurched. He hadn't noticed Keal on the floor because a chunk of wallboard was lying on top of him.

Xander knelt beside him. "Keal?" He shoved the piece of wall off the man and rolled him over onto his back.

David ran up. "Is he—"

Xander leaned in close. His fingers pushed against Keal's neck, checking the carotid artery for a pulse. "He's alive." He touched a gash on Keal's head, showed David the blood. "Hasn't dried, not even a little."

Toward the far end of the hall, a door slammed. David jumped and looked into the hall's shadows. "That was a *portal* door," he whispered.

Xander scowled. "Phemus," he said. "Taking off."

"Taking off? More likely coming back."

Xander scrambled to his feet and backed toward the landing. "Come on, Dae," he whispered.

But David leaned over Keal and touched his cheek. "Keal?" he whispered. "Keal!"

The guy was out. David hopped over Keal's head, stooped to grab one wrist, and tugged. "Xander, help."

His brother grabbed Keal's other wrist. "David, we don't have time for this," he said. They heaved back, dragging Keal six inches. "This guy weighs—"

A door at the end of the hall opened. Yellowish light from the antechamber spilled out. A shadow moved through it.

"Hide!" Xander whispered.

They lowered Keal's arms and rushed on tiptoe to the landing. They descended a few stairs, and David grabbed Xander's shoulder.

"We can't leave him," he said. He couldn't stand the thought of Keal lost . . . over *there*, in time, possibly for years.

"If Phemus wanted him," Xander said, "he'd already be gone. Anyway, what are *we* supposed to do? We've already tried stopping Phemus when he came for Mom."

*And look how that ended up,* David thought. *Mom gone, all three King men banged up, bruised, and bloody.*

He heard stomping in the third-floor hallway, crunching over the debris. He didn't like it, but Xander was right: there was nothing they could do. David wanted to help, despite the odds, but the family couldn't handle another of them kidnapped, seriously injured, or killed—one of which was nearly certain if they challenged Phemus.

Xander pulled at David's elbow. David nodded, and his brother led the way down the third-floor stairs, staying close to the outside edge so the treads wouldn't creak. David listened to the footsteps approach.

When David was at the bottom of the stairs, the footsteps on the third floor stopped—right where Keal was, it seemed to David. He thought he was going to be sick.

Xander grabbed David again and pulled him through the doors in the two walls that separated this secret area from the main part of the house. They stopped, listening. Up on the third floor, Phemus's footsteps clomped on the landing.

"He's coming down," David whispered.

Xander said, "We have to get out of the house."

As David followed him to the corner where the main hallway met this shorter one, he realized the footsteps behind him didn't sound quite right. Something was off, but he couldn't figure out what it was.

Xander cut diagonally across the hall to the main staircase, which would take them to the foyer and the front door.

Behind them, the footsteps were coming down the third-floor stairs.

Xander hit the first step of the main staircase and braked. David bumped into him. The airy first letter of "Hey!" was on his lips when he saw what had stopped his brother: Phemus was not behind them. He was standing right there in the foyer.

FRIDAY, 10:51 A.M.

*If Phemus is in the foyer,* David thought, *who just came out of the portal?*

The big man hadn't noticed the boys at the top of the stairs. His back was to them, and he stared out the window beside the front door. He was so tall, he had to stoop to do it. His scarred and dirty back rose and fell as he took slow, deep breaths.

Whoever had come out of the portal reached the bottom of the third-floor stairs.

David darted past the banister overlooking the foyer, toward his bedroom. Xander was practically glued to his back. David's foot struck the chair that had been propped against the linen closet door, but now blocked the center of the hall. The chair scraped on the hardwood floor, sounding to David like a loud cough.

In the foyer, Phemus grunted. His gravely baritone filled the air: *"Poios einai ekei?"* And he began climbing the stairs.

David's heart slammed into his throat, apparently trying to exit the body that was ten seconds from getting pummeled to death. His eyes flashed at Xander and he pointed to the linen closet door: *Let's go through!*

Xander shook his head. He grabbed David's arm and pulled him backward into the dark bathroom. The boys stepped into the tub and slowly pulled the shower curtain. Each plastic hook seemed to *scream* a grinding protest along the metal rod.

David kept patting the air with his hand, telling Xander to *be quiet!*

When the curtain fully shielded them, David whispered, "The closet, Xander. Why not the closet?"

"No time," Xander said. "I'm not going through *with* you, and I'm not waiting around while *you* go through."

They had already had that discussion, the one that conjured the image of their bodies melding into one hideous mass on the other side.

Voices in the hallway: someone whispered, Phemus rumbled

out a reply in that strange language Wuzzy had captured. It seemed so foreign to David's ears, it hurt to hear it.

David rose on his tiptoes to less-than-whisper in Xander's ear. "If that wasn't Phemus upstairs, who was it?"

Xander put his finger over his lips again, hushing him.

Footsteps came down the hall, quiet, slow. The way the stranger had whispered, and now the stealthy inspection— David was sure the intruders suspected someone else was in the house.

David focused on not shifting his weight, for fear of making the tub creak. He knew Xander was doing the same. He tried to slow his breathing, but that wasn't going to happen. He opened his mouth wide, thinking it would give the air more room to be quiet.

An idea occurred to him: the best thing to do was to jump through the shower curtain, screaming like a wild man, and simply plow through the men in the hall. He could do it. Just today, he'd faced a Confederate assault, a torturer, and Hannibal's entire Carthaginian army. What were two men? All he and Xander had to do was surprise them long enough to slam past and run out the front door. That's all . . .

But one of them was Phemus, a brute so massive he was less like a man than a walking wall with fists. The other was probably one of his equally big and nasty brethren. Trying to run past them would be like a Nintendo game—Mario diving into a passageway of cutting blades, falling boulders, and fire-breathing dragons. It usually took a few bloody deaths to figure it out, and in real life David had only one to give.

*What was I thinking?*

In the hall, a floorboard creaked.

David grabbed a handful of his brother's shirt and closed his eyes.

The footsteps passed the bathroom, disappeared into their bedroom. Somebody else moved in the hall, quietly lifting the chair and setting it down. The first person walked out of the bedroom and into the spare room. The other crept back toward the staircase, maybe intending to check out Toria's room, then Mom and Dad's.

The first man came back into the hall. He said something. It was Phemus, that rumbly gibberish. His footsteps moved to the bathroom door.

*No one in here,* David thought, concentrating with all his mental energy to *push* the words into Phemus's head. *Just an empty bathroom. Walk on by.*

It worked! Phemus walked on.

For some unknown reason—excitement, relief, a twitch— David's left foot turned just a little: *squeeeeak.*

Phemus stopped moving. When he started again, it was to return to the bathroom.

The light flicked on.

CHAPTER

# forty-nine

"I really appreciate your seeing me like this, Mike," Ed King said.

He sat in a chair in front of the desk of his old friend. He looked over his shoulder at Toria, who was gazing in wonder at the artifacts arrayed on bookcases, in display cases, and mounted on the walls. There were masks, maps, and fragments of ancient papyri. Volumes and volumes of books, some of which Mike had authored.

Ed looked at his friend, hitched a thumb toward Toria, and whispered, "She's a good kid. She won't touch anything."

Mike Peterson waved his hand dismissively. "I'm sure of it. Who knows? Maybe she'll catch the bug, want to spend her life unraveling the secrets of ancient languages."

"Maybe," Toria said politely.

Located in Dodd Hall on the UCLA campus, the Department of Classics boasted experts in all the subfields of philology: paleography, classical linguistics, Byzantine studies, medieval Latin . . . Ed couldn't even remember all of them, and at the moment, he didn't care. He had come to find out about only one language, spoken by one person—Phemus.

He pushed his hands into the overnight bag on the floor and pulled out Wuzzy.

Mike smiled when he saw the bear. "Okay . . ." he said. He pushed away mounds of paper on his desk.

Ed positioned Wuzzy on the clean spot of desktop, facing Mike. He fiddled with the controls on the back.

"Wait," Mike said, holding up his hand. "Before I hear it again, what can you tell me about the speaker?"

"Almost nothing," Ed said. "I can give you a physical description, but it may not be pertinent."

Mike nodded. He leaned across the desk, closed his eyes, and turned his ear toward the bear. "Go ahead."

CHAPTER

David trembled, much as he had in the freezing Alps, but this time with fear.

A huge shadow moved on the other side of the shower curtain, like a whale under the surface of the ocean. The floor creaked under Phemus's feet.

Xander was looking around. David knew what he wanted: a weapon, something to protect themselves. But they were standing in a tub! They could use the curtain rod, maybe, but Phemus would probably snatch it out of Xander's hands, eat it, and continue to the main course of King-Kid Fricassee.

David reached to the back edge of the tub and picked up a bottle of shampoo. He positioned his thumb to pop it open as soon as he had to.

*Go for the eyes,* he thought. *Smear it in. Better than nothing.*

The other man called from somewhere down the hallway. It sounded like *"Zikor"*—and David recognized the voice: Taksidian! No wonder his footsteps sounded wrong. When the man who had exited the antechamber had come down the third-floor stairs, David had pictured barefooted Phemus.

The big man turned. His broad shoulder caught the curtain, pushing it open. David and Xander stood exposed, staring at Phemus's back. The man lumbered to the doorway. One dinner-plate-sized hand pressed against the wall above the door; the other gripped the frame. He leaned through. *"Mas teleionoyn?"*

Phemus went through, turned, and disappeared. His thumping feet, the creaking of the floor moved away down the hall.

Taksidian whispered, a barely audible mumble. Then his booted feet descended the main staircase.

David whispered, "That's Taksidian. He's using the portals when we're not here."

Xander nodded. He lifted his leg over the side of the tub and stepped out.

David reached out, tapped him, and furiously shook his head: *no!*

Xander gave him a thumbs-up. He walked slowly to the door.

David stepped out, knowing he was going to trip or knock something over or otherwise give themselves away.

Xander leaned his head through the doorway. David looked around his brother.

Phemus was standing at the top of the stairs, gazing down at the foyer. The front door opened, filling the air with sunlight. It slammed closed. Phemus sighed and trudged slowly toward the back hall.

Xander pulled back into the bathroom. He grabbed David's shoulder; the excitement in his eyes sent a chill over David's skin. His brother whispered, "This is it, our big chance."

"For *what*?"

"To follow him. All we have to do—"

"Follow him?" David jerked back. "What's wrong with you? I thought—"

"Shhh, shhh," Xander said. "Hear me out." He jabbed a thumb toward Phemus. "He's heading home, *his* home—*where he took Mom!* Somehow, he goes in and out without using the antechamber items. We'll never know where he goes unless we go with him."

David batted Xander's hand off his shoulder. This was crazy talk, as bad as David taking on the torturer. He said,

"We *will* find out where he's from. Without doing this! Dad's with that professor right now. He's—"

"He's only *hoping* the guy can tell him where Phemus came from," Xander said. "How close do you think he'll get to pinpointing the very place, the very time . . . a hundred possibilities? A thousand?" He peered around the corner, came back. "We can find out *for sure*, the *exact* place, the *exact* time. No messing around. Dae, if *he* can come and go, we can too. We'll slip through right after him, take a look around, and come right back."

David bit his lip. "I don't know."

"I *do*. Mom might still be there. Once we know what world it is, we can focus on it, find a way to get back, keep looking for her there."

David closed his eyes. Xander was making sense. Dangerous sense, but sense.

"And think about it," Xander said. "We'll probably figure out what we need to keep Phemus out. If that's the only thing we learn, it's a lot."

"But Xander," David said, "*now?* We just hit three worlds. I hurt everywhere. I'm beat, more than I ever have been."

"It has to be now." Xander leaned past him, opened the medicine cupboard behind the mirror, and took out a bottle. He popped off the top. "Here."

David held out his hand, and Xander tapped two Tylenol into it.

Xander stepped out of the bathroom and turned back. "I have to do this, Dae," he whispered. "With or without you."

David wanted to punch him. His brother knew David wouldn't let him go alone, not after Jesse told them to stay together, not after all the times they'd survived only because the other was there.

Xander moved down the hall, fast and quiet. David moaned to himself. He tossed the pills into his mouth, slipped into the hall, and hurried to catch up.

CHAPTER

Friday, 11:00 a.m.

After Phemus's last syllable came out of Wuzzy's speaker, Mike Peterson didn't move. He held his position—ear angled toward the bear, eyes closed—for a good twenty seconds. Finally he leaned back and looked at Ed. His fingers pushed into his lips, which slowly spread out behind them into a smile. He said, "This is rich."

"What is?" Ed said, hopefully. "Do you recognize it?"

"Not precisely. But I can tell you it's a language no one alive has ever heard, let alone *speaks*." He leaned forward, grinning. "Who put you up to this? Was it Jackson? I didn't know you two knew each other."

"I don't understand," Ed said.

Toria came up beside him, put her hand on his arm.

Mike pointed at Wuzzy. "It's very good. Technically perfect. Of course, people have argued about the precise phonology for . . . well, forever."

Ed blinked a few times, trying to follow. "So, you know it . . . or not?"

Mike frowned. He leaned back in his chair. "The general epoch, not the exact culture."

Ed felt his shoulders sag.

Toria said, "That's all right, Daddy."

Ed asked Mike, "Is there *any* way to pin it down?"

Mike squinted at him. "This isn't a joke? Not Jackson? Kuiper?"

Dad held his hand up. "Mike, I assure you this is not a joke. Look, even if you think it is, do me a favor. Tell me what language it is . . . please."

Mike stared at him a long time, seeming to consider whether to play along. Finally he adjusted himself in his chair and said, "Let me show you something." He gripped a computer monitor on the side of his desk and rotated it so all of them could see it.

"Some colleagues of mine—philologists at universities all over the world—have been working on a computer program. We built a massive database of known and even rumored languages. Our goal is to identify written language instantly, no matter when or where it was used. In other words, we scan a bit of an ancient manuscript or a photo of pictograms on a cave wall, and the computer will tell us, for example, that it's proto-Canaanite or whatever. Sort of like the FBI's computerized database of fingerprints, but with language."

He grinned, obviously excited. "A side project that a few of us have been developing is the application of phoneme inventories to the writing. It attempts to apply syllable structure, stress, accent, intonation . . . the rules database is enormous. I mean just the phonotactics alone . . ."

*Come on, come on,* Ed thought. *I just want to find my wife. Can you help me or not?* He tried to smile when Mike looked at him, but he knew his frustration was showing.

"I'm sorry," Mike said. "It means the computer can *speak* the written language we feed it, regardless of how long ago the last speaker lived." He opened a drawer, pulled out a microphone, and started unraveling its cord. "Now, here's the part you came for: we can reverse the process to make it turn spoken language into writing, which it will then identify." He plugged the microphone into the computer and held it up to Wuzzy, as though the bear were a celebrity on a red carpet.

Mike said, "Let's hear it again."

CHAPTER

FRIDAY, AT THE SAME TIME

Xander reached the shorter hallway and shot a glance around the corner. He held up his fist, commando-style, telling David to stop.

David heard Phemus's footsteps—going through the space between the walls.

Xander turned. "We're going to have to move fast," he said, his voice low. "We have to get through the door after Phemus, but before it closes. Stay with me." He swung around the corner.

David grabbed his arm. "What happens on the *other side?*" he said. "We're going to run right into him."

"We get away from him," Xander said.

As far as David was concerned, he might as well have said, *Don't let the grenade go off in your hands.* Except Phemus was scarier than a grenade.

Xander rushed to the doorless secret passage through the wall, then slipped through.

David realized he was still holding the bottle of shampoo. He shoved it into his back pocket and hurried to the space between the walls. Xander was peering around the edge of the second door. Phemus's footsteps echoed near the top of the stairs.

*Don't take Keal,* David thought. *Don't take him, don't hurt him anymore.* If Phemus tried either, they would have to stop him—somehow. He had an image of them stepping into the third-floor hallway with Phemus standing there, expecting them, holding Keal high over his head, ready to throw him like a log.

Without looking, Xander patted David's arm and stepped through the doorway. He went up, planting only the toes of his sneakers on each tread. David moved right behind him. His arm throbbed, a dull pulse followed by a sharp knife-stab. He tried not to think about what it felt like: the edge of his broken bone slipping up into his muscles.

At the landing, Xander looked into the crooked hallway. He duckwalked into it. David followed, then stopped. Phemus was in the hallway, plodding toward the far end.

*If he looks back . . .*

Xander kept going, passing Keal and actually closing in on the brute. David supposed they couldn't wait until Phemus was completely in the antechamber, but this seemed . . . the word *careless* came to mind, but he wasn't sure it expressed what he thought, that they were jabbing a stick at a mean and hungry lion.

*Oh, right: stupid*—that's the word he was looking for.

Staying low, David waddled past Keal, snagged his leg on something, and fell forward. He landed on his palms, locking his arms to keep from going all the way to the floor, which certainly would have made enough noise to draw Phemus's attention. He turned to find Keal's hand around his ankle.

The man was lifting his head, looking at him with groggy eyes. He moved his lips to say something.

David reached back and covered Keal's mouth. He leaned in close. "Shhh," he said and glanced down the hall. Phemus stepped into an antechamber. Xander was five feet behind. "We're following him," David whispered. "Phemus. Back to his world."

Keal's eyes sprung wide. He mumbled through David's hand and shook his head.

"Shhh," David repeated. "We have to."

Xander slipped into the antechamber. His shadow cut a trembling black hole in the bright light coming out of the room and splashing on the opposite wall.

David spun away from Keal, pulling his ankle free. Behind him, Keal wheezed, "Wait . . . David . . . *no.*"

At the antechamber door, David looked back. Keal was staring at him, pushing himself up, shaking his head. Weakly, the man called his name.

David stepped in. Xander was in front of the portal door, which radiated with chilly air. Beyond, light swirled through blackness, like cream hitting the surface of a cup of coffee.

"Hurry," Xander said. He held something out for David to take. It was a long stick with what looked like the pointed tine of a deer antler strapped to one end: a spear. "Just in case we need it to get back."

David noticed the other items in the room: a chunk of rock that might have been a blunt arrowhead; a cluster of straw, tied at one end; and a leather pouch with something inside. They were different items from the ones in the antechamber when Mom was taken. Then, there had been a fur-lined parka, goggles, gloves . . . and snow had blown in. But they had always thought Phemus had taken Mom someplace else, that the antechamber items had nothing to do with where she had ended up, because somehow Phemus didn't need the items to open the door.

David grabbed his brother's shirt, and they fell through. The door swung shut, banging into David's butt, giving them a fierce shove.

CHAPTER

# fifty-three

Shadows churned around David, forming into a cave. A long, rock-lined tunnel came into view, lit by the portal itself. David braced himself to touch down . . . but he never did. He felt a great force jerking him back, flipping him sideways.

As frightened as he had been before, a new level of fear clutched him. The portals had never been like this: violent and . . . *unsure*. That's what it felt like, that it was unsure where it was taking them.

He spilled down onto Xander. Sunlight cut into his eyes, as though someone had yanked away thick curtains just as he was waking from a deep sleep. He slipped off Xander onto a hard floor. He pulled in a deep breath to gasp or scream or cry out.

His brother clutched his head, put his face right into David's, said, "Shh." The sound was fast, sharp, and quiet. Coupled with Xander's panicked eyes, he knew: they were someplace where any noise at all would be very, very bad.

He remembered: they'd come through just seconds after Phemus.

Xander swiveled his head around quickly. David looked past him to see Phemus across a room, heading for a door. The big man stopped, tilted his head, as though he'd caught a sound.

Xander shoved David and rolled away. They were in a sort of cubby or alcove off the room. A large pillar rose from the floor on either side of the alcove's opening. David got it: he rolled behind one, pulling his legs up, as Phemus started to turn around. Xander did the same behind the other pillar.

Seconds passed, then the door opened and closed. Xander looked around the pillar. He leaned his head back and let out a long breath.

David stretched out, covered his eyes with his hand. "What just happened?" he said.

"David, move!" Xander said.

The wall beside David, a huge slab of rock, was trembling.

He rolled away, toward his brother's reaching hands. His finger scraped over grooves in the stone floor. They arched from the corner of the trembling wall to the portal they had just come through. He understood, and realized he was still in the way.

Following the grooves, the rock wall swung toward him like a door. It was going to catch his hip, pinning him between it and the portal. If it carried the same force as the portal doors in the antechambers, it would crush him, cut him in half. He yelled.

Xander grabbed his arm and pulled. The wall struck David's foot, like the bumper of a speeding car. His legs flipped out of the way, and the wall completed its quarter-circle movement. It rumbled against the portal, completely covering it.

David pulled his foot up and rubbed it through the sneaker. He hissed at the tenderness of it.

Xander stared, biting his lip.

"It's all right," David assured him, easing his foot to the floor. "I've taken worse in soccer games."

Xander turned to the slab of wall. "It's like at home," he said. "A door over a portal."

"What opens it?" David said, because wasn't that the most important thing they needed to know? If that was the portal home, how did they get to it?

Xander stood. He tugged at the rock door. It didn't budge.

"Xander," David said, pointing at items mounted to the

stone wall above and around the door: a plank of wood, a strip of the same wallpaper that decorated the upstairs hallway, a dirty doorknob, other things—all arranged around the door like the symbols he'd seen etched in the doorframes of ancient temples.

"Stuff from our house," Xander said, eyeing each one carefully. "That must be how they're doing it. Somehow they locked the portal in place, keeping it linked to the house, with these things."

"And this area," David said, looking around the alcove. "It's like a stone version of an antechamber."

Xander brushed past him, out of the alcove. David pushed off the floor, then remembered: he scanned the area around him, feeling his pulse pick up speed. "Xander . . . the spear. I lost it."

Xander turned back. "Where?"

"I don't know," David said, feeling panicky. "It must have been when we were in that cave. The pull tugged us away. I must have dropped it then."

Xander said, "Don't worry about it."

"Don't—? How are we going to get home?"

His brother nodded toward the big stone door. "The portal's right there. I bet Phemus just strolls right into our house whenever he wants to."

"But it's huge. What if we can't open it?"

Xander smiled. He pulled something out of his pocket and

held it up. It was a woven tassel, like something people attached car keys to or girls put in their hair.

"What is it?"

"I don't know, but it's from the antechamber," Xander said. "I got it before you came in. One way or another, we'll get home." He tied the tassel to a belt loop. "There. Now we can see when the pull starts."

"*If* it starts," David said. "We're not in that cave the portal sent us to. Somehow, Phemus opened another portal *on top of* that one—and brought us here."

Xander frowned and looked at the tassel. "We'll see, I guess. I got this from the antechamber too." He dug a stone out of his pocket. It was shiny silver, like a gold nugget's poor cousin. He returned it to his pocket and said, "It's the best we can do, Dae. We've never been stuck in a world . . . yet."

*Yet,* David thought. *Did he have to say that?*

The room beyond the antechamber was about the size of a two-car garage. A table and chairs occupied the area to the right of the alcove. Behind them, a bed squatted against the wall. Its frame was rough wood, showing hack marks from whatever tool had shaped it. Layers of woven blankets made it look comfortable. Light came in from glassless slits in the wall, like the ones David had seen in pictures of castles.

Xander walked over to what looked like a towel hanging on the wall. He took it down and tossed it to David. "Try this on."

It was a short tunic, dingy white and soft. David slipped it over his head and cinched a braided rope around his waist. The belt and skirtlike hem disguised the fact that it was too big for him—except that it had no sleeves, and the armholes came to his bottom ribs. He adjusted Xander's belt, which looped over his chest, and put his left arm through it. "Much better," he said. "I don't feel so naked."

"You look like you belong," Xander said. "Better than me."

"I guess that depends on where we are. Any idea?"

"One way to find out." Xander cracked the door open a few inches. He stuck his face to the opening, then threw back the door. He and David stepped out onto a stone terrace. Hedges framed the area, and beyond them, lush green grass rode a long, sloping hill down to what appeared to be docks and a river that must have been at least a half mile wide. Dense forests grew on either side of the hill.

David swept his vision beyond the river and gasped.

CHAPTER

# fifty-four

Keal felt half asleep. He shook his head and grimaced at the
pain he felt, as though a cannonball were banging around inside
his skull. He kept his eyes on the open doorway David had
gone through, the way he'd been taught to lock his gaze on the
place a drowning man went under, while swimming for it. He
crawled down the hallway.

*Those kids are following Phemus! Are they nuts?*

Phemus was a machine made out of muscle. And when he had to, the guy knew how to move. Keal had learned that the hard way. He had been working on the walls at the base of the stairs when he'd heard a noise. He'd stepped into the hall to investigate, and Phemus had pounced. Keal thought he'd given as good as he got, but in the end, it was Keal who'd wound up unconscious on the floor.

Now Xander and David were going after him, like poodles taking on a dragon.

Keal arrived at the antechamber, pulled himself up by the frame, and stumbled in. The portal door was shut, locked. He tugged on it anyway, then spun to the items. He reached for a pouch hanging from a hook. A wave of dizziness washed over him, and the cannonball bumped into the inside of his forehead. He dropped a knee onto the bench, pressed a palm against the wall.

*Come on, come on,* he thought.

The image of the boys trying to duck away from Phemus's swinging fists forced his eyes open. He snatched the pouch down from the hook, grabbed the two other items—a small bundle of hay and a rock—and yanked the portal door open.

CHAPTER

fifty-five

"Okay," Mike Peterson said. "It's scanning the databases now."

Ed leaned forward to get a better view of the monitor. Flickering letters and words faded to black. A small dot appeared in the middle and expanded until a globe filled the screen. Ed recognized the American continents, hosting the countries of Canada, the US, all the way down to Chile and Argentina. The globe began a slow rotation toward Europe.

Words flashed in the top left corner: *Indo-European . . . Celtic . . . Germanic . . . Greek . . .* The top right corner showed years counting backward by century: *AD 2000 . . . AD 1900 . . . AD 1800 . . .* As the words and years changed, geopolitical boundaries shrank and expanded, appeared and disappeared over the image of land masses. The globe rotated one way, then the other. It zoomed in, back out, zoomed in again. The program isolated certain areas, appeared to change its mind, and zipped to another location.

Back and back the years went: *AD 100 . . . AD 1 . . . 100 BC . . .* At 600 BC, the location hovered over the Greek islands, then began moving west. It settled over the Atlantic Ocean, zooming in on the Azores Islands.

Mike nodded. "I thought so."

On the screen, the small group of nine islands melted into one large island and continued to expand, as if rising out of the ocean.

When the computer let out a musical chime, Ed jumped. Nothing more on the screen moved. Then a label appeared over the new landmass.

Ed stared at it for at least ten seconds. He looked at Mike out of the corner of his eye. He said, "You've got to be kidding."

CHAPTER

fifty-six

David stared in awe.

The land on the other side of the river was a huge mountain that climbed high above them. At the peak was a castle or fortress many times larger than any he had ever seen. The shape, as well, was peculiar: every wall was straight, but they jutted one way and then another, as though the builders had followed the shape of the mountaintop in order to make the structure as large as the plateau would allow. At every juncture where the walls took a turn, towers rose above the level of the parapets. Spaced evenly along the top perimeter were flags of every color, shape, and design, hundreds of them fluttering in the wind. But the most striking aspect of the castle—for David had decided it was definitely a king's castle—was its color: the entire thing appeared to be covered in or made out of gold. Sunlight glinted from it in a thousand places.

Below the castle, cliffs dropped a short distance to smaller buildings. These structures appeared to have been constructed of polished rock: black, silver, and red, all glistening as though wet. Some were checkered, others striped, and a few cobbled together with no discernable pattern. They seemed to follow an avenue—about the width of a football field—that gently spiraled around the mountain, climbing toward the top. Two levels down from the castle, a bridge spanned a broad crevasse, allowing the avenue to continue. Tall pillars and arches supported the bridge. They were so ornately carved, David thought Michelangelo must have had a hand in their design. The bridge, arches, and pillars were made out of the same blood-red stone, polished to mirror perfection.

The buildings flanked the bridge, but did not encroach on it. Rather, the bridge's surface had been turned into a park: except for a strip of road on its inside edge, grass covered it. Big trees grew straight up from it. The space below was too shadowy for David to see where the root systems went.

People were enjoying it as they would any park. Some were

picnicking, others strolling hand in hand. Children rolled and tussled. One boy flew a kite, a dragon-shaped collection of colorful fabric that rose higher than the rooftops of the buildings on the next level up. Roving musicians danced as they played their instruments, which David could *almost* hear in the movements of the musicians' bodies.

A ribbon of water, as wide as a street, fell from an arched opening at the base of the castle. It disappeared behind the buildings on the highest level, then emerged from beneath another structure and fell to the level below. It did that two more times before reaching the foot of the mountain. There it became a stream that ran through a large garden of trimmed hedges and topiary, where more people strolled, musicians played, and gymnasts and jesters performed. Eventually the stream drained into the large river that separated David from the spectacular mountain-city.

"Xander," David said, breathless. "It's . . ."

"Beautiful," Xander said. "Incredible."

"Let's get over there," David said.

"Yeah . . . *no!*" Xander said. "We're not here for that."

*Of course not,* David thought. But eyeing the glittering gold and polished stone, the fantastic buildings and flawless . . . *bushes*—for crying out loud!—he wanted to be there. He ached to experience it, to walk in the parks, taste the food, and listen to the music, which he was certain would change his idea of what music could be.

"No, I . . . wow," David said. "I've never heard of a place like this. Where . . . *when* . . . are we?"

"Come on," Xander said. He led David off the side of the terrace, where a cobblestone path led around the house and down a steep hill, in the other direction from the grassy slope to the river. The path had been carved into the earth, forming vine-covered cliffs that rose on either side.

"I can smell the ocean," David said. "Salty."

Xander crinkled his nose. "And something not so nice."

"I thought that was you," David said and laughed.

Xander gave him a shove. He said, "When we get to wherever this path leads, keep your eyes open for Phemus."

They rounded a bend, and David saw that the path ended at a tall metal gate. It was intricately designed, with swooping curls of iron and ornamental flowers, petals, and leaves. At its center, framed by two concentric circles, a crown rested on a smaller circle, as though on a faceless head. A few feet beyond the gate, a wall of leaves showed that the carved-out path hooked sharply to the right.

Xander fiddled with a lever and sprang the gate open.

Stepping through, David took in the gate's beautiful craftsmanship. He shook his head. "I can't imagine him coming from a place like this."

But that impression ended when they turned with the path and stepped into a large town square.

CHAPTER

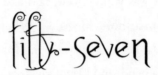

fifty-seven

Keal crashed down onto hard, uneven ground. Stretching out before him, illuminated by light pouring in from the portal behind him, was a tunnel. The irregular angles of its walls made him think it was naturally formed, by a stream or water that had once cut through the earth around him.

The portal door slammed shut, plunging him into darkness. The door's sound echoed down the tunnel, as though scurrying to get away.

"Xander?" he called. "David?" His voice bounced against the walls and faded away. He sat in the darkness, thinking.

The items from the antechamber. They always had something to do with the world beyond the portal. He set the straw and stone down and reached his hand into the pouch. It was full of round stones that made him think of marbles. What he needed were matches.

*Of course . . .*

He got to his knees and picked up the straw and stone. He pushed the straw into the stone floor of the cave and hammered the stone down. It sparked against the floor. He did it again and again, until an orange dot appeared on a piece of straw. It flared into a flame, igniting the straw around it. He raised the burning bundle by one end, which had been wrapped tightly with a strip of leather.

A torch instead of a flashlight. A piece of flint instead of matches. He had a feeling the portal had sent him back in time a long, *long* way.

The fire cast a weak yellow glow that showed him only the tunnel walls nearest him. He turned on his knees and saw blackness in both directions.

He laid his hand over his throbbing head and rubbed it.

"Xander?" he called again. "David?"

He spotted something on the ground next to the curving wall. A spear. He picked it up and stood.

"Xander! David!"

The tunnel mocked him, repeating and swallowing his words: "David . . . David . . . David . . ."

He stared into the nothingness in each direction. *Which way?* Something on the wall caught his eye, and he waved the flame in front of it: a cave painting. It depicted two men fighting a bear-like creature as big as an elephant. Unlike the cave paintings he'd seen in history books, it wasn't faded or chipped. This one was *new.*

*Oh, please,* he thought. *Don't tell me I'm in prehistoric times. Don't tell me that!*

He began walking, calling the boys' names.

A noise stopped him. It was an echo weaving through the echo of his own voice. He stood perfectly still and listened. Like music through the walls of a house, the sound reached him, a slow, pulsating whisper: breathing.

"Xander?" he said. "David?" But he knew this deep, heavy breathing didn't come from one of them. The echoing made it impossible to guess how near it was, the source of this sound. He couldn't even be sure from which direction it came.

Then something in the darkness ahead scraped against stone, and the breathing grew louder. The thing snorted, loud as a train shooting out a quick blast of steam.

Keal lifted the spear and started backing away.

CHAPTER

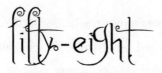

David gaped at the barbaric chaos splayed out in front of him and Xander.

The open-front stalls of tradesmen and vendors formed a crescent around the square, broken here and there to accommodate animal corrals. As much as the mountain-city was dazzling and alluring, the marketplace spread out before them was ugly and repulsive.

To their immediate right, a blacksmith pounded on metal,

setting the teeth-grinding tone of the place: *Clang! Clang! Clang!* In front of the smith, burly men examined knives and swords, spiked clubs and spears. They swung them at each other and at passersby, laughing and shouting. David could not understand their language, but by their sneers and the sharp sounds of their words, he guessed their talk was vulgar and abusive. Similar words rang out throughout the square.

He pushed the hair off his forehead and kept his palm pressed against his head. The assault on his senses made his brain ache.

In one stall a man cut the heads off fish, sliced into their bellies, and yanked out their guts. He slung the stuff onto the square's cobblestones, where people clomped over the bloody piles. Another vendor butchered chickens, letting their headless bodies run around until they fell over. The market appeared to be dedicated to food, drink, weapons, and armor.

At the center of the square, two bare-chested men battered each other, while others cheered them on. One swung his fist into the face of the other, who staggered back, spewing blood. He wiped his nose with the back of his hand, smiled a toothless grin, and retaliated with a frenzy of wild punches.

As though sprayed into this bedlam as some psycho artist's final touch, an odor wafted over David—a offensive fusion of manure, raw meat, sweat, and things David didn't want to think about.

"Xander?" David said, gripping the hem of his brother's T-shirt. He looked back at the path. The house that had admitted them into this world appeared to be situated on a hill that marked this side of the square. To their left, a wide street cut into the same hill. Past that, buildings sprung up and arched around, making a huge circle out of what he had thought of as a "town square."

Xander said, "See anything that indicates where we are?"

"Hell?" David suggested.

His brother nodded. "The road continues on the other side," he said. "Maybe it leads to someplace . . . more sane."

"What about that way?" David said. He pointed left, where a wide opening between the nearest buildings revealed more structures on the other side of the square.

"Docks, I think," Xander said. "See the masts?"

And then David did. Tall poles rose behind the buildings and stalls. Crossbeams held gathered folds of canvas sails.

They started walking, giving wide berth to rowdy men. As they went deeper into the square, they could see more of the ships to their left: at least two of them docked in a line.

"David," Xander said. He was looking into one of the corrals coming up on their right.

First David saw the men, sitting on the top rails of the fence, whooping and hollering with excitement. Next, he saw what captured their attention: boys younger than himself were going at each other with more ferocity than the men in the center of the square. A dozen or more of them punched, kicked, clawed, and bit. One tumbled away from the melee, staggered to his feet, shook his head, and dived back in.

David was accustomed to roughhousing with friends, even little skirmishes with school bullies—this was something completely different. Unless he misread their expressions and the force of their fighting, these kids wanted to kill each other.

As if to confirm this, one of the men pitched a club onto the ground near the boys. Another tossed something that glinted as it spun in the air. A boy spotted the club and went for it.

David turned away and walked faster. He laid a hand over his stomach, afraid he would puke on the spot, not that anyone would notice or that the mess would make the square any fouler than it was.

"How can *this* place be so close to that beautiful mountain?" he said. "I don't get it."

"Just keep walking," Xander said.

A commotion drew David's eyes to the dock road. Men walked into the square, presumably from one of the ships. They were dressed like soldiers with thick leather vests, arm guards, and greaves covering their knees and shins. Using swords, spears, and whips, they herded a large group of prisoners, the sight of which froze David's breath. They were nearly identical to Phemus: massive, dressed only in pelts, crazy eyes flashing around. Each was bound in a wooden stock that clamped around his neck and projected beyond his shoulders, where his wrists were also locked in place. Chains looped from stock to stock, keeping them all together. They shuffled, tripped, and lurched along under the constant bite of the soldiers' weapons.

David backed into his brother.

The soldiers prodded their prisoners toward another corral. Inside were more of the Phemus-like brutes, all in stocks, bumping into each other, glancing around with glazed expressions. A few were more animated than the others, bouncing, chattering like hyenas. David focused on one of them and elbowed Xander in the ribs.

"Hey . . ." Xander said.

"That one closest to us, in the corral!" David said. "Isn't that—?"

"Monkey Man," Xander finished. He was one of the two other men who had come out of the portal with Phemus while Xander was putting up the camera in the third-floor hallway. Smaller than the rest, he seemed to make up for his puniness with a fidgety aggression that had scared the tar out of David back in the house. The creature had balanced like a gargoyle on Phemus's shoulder, then hurled himself down the staircase at the boys. David could make out the man's bruised and battered face now—evidence that he was indeed the one who'd slammed into the door as they tried to close it, the one David had smacked on the head with the butt of the toy rifle.

A deep voice came from behind them: "He's a little worse for wear, isn't he?"

The boys spun and found themselves facing Taksidian.

# fifty-nine

Taksidian glared at them, a sly smile playing on his lips. His kinky black hair vibrated in the light breeze, dancing against the collar of his black trench coat.

David quickly checked the man's hands for weapons, but they were empty. After all, what did the guy need one for? His deadliest weapon hovered behind him: Phemus. The brute stared pure hatred into David. His shoulders pumped up and down with the bellows of his lungs. The beard around his mouth parted to show a snarling mouth of canted and broken teeth.

Xander slapped his hand into David's chest, seizing his tunic. He turned and started to run.

Taksidian sidestepped, and Phemus lurched in. He grabbed each boy by a wrist and hoisted them into the air. David kicked him in the ribs, over and over, all the while squirming and wiggling to get free. But Phemus's flanks were rock solid and his hand like a vise that embraced most of David's forearm.

Xander hissed and spat like a wild animal. He clawed at Phemus's arm. The man merely grinned.

"Let go!" David wailed. He looked into Taksidian's passive face and said, "You can't do this!"

But of course David knew he could, especially in a place like this. A quick glance around revealed no concerned faces; hardly anyone at all was watching, and those who were seemed to enjoy the entertainment.

Taksidian raised his hand and called out. *"Froyres, edo parakalo!"*

Three of the soldiers broke away from the group of prisoners and trotted toward them.

"This seems like your kind of place," Xander said. "Why don't you just stay here and leave us alone?"

"Oh, I would," Taksidian said. "But you know it isn't going to be around much longer. It—"

Something he saw in Xander's expression made him stop.

He turned to David and smiled at the bewilderment David knew his face reflected.

Taksidian laughed. "You mean, you haven't figured out where you are?" He held his arm wide and looked around at the square. "Gentlemen, welcome to Atlantis!"

Xander scowled in disbelief. "What?" he said. "The *lost continent?*"

"That's a myth," David said.

Taksidian's eyebrows went up. "So is time travel, right? Now you know better." He smiled. "So you see why I wouldn't want to make this my permanent home. As Plato reported, a tidal wave wipes it out in a single day and night." He examined his wrist, as if checking a watch that wasn't there. "And that time is fast approaching. Besides, Atlantis already has enough kings, a consortium of them, in fact. I could never be one of them. I could never have the power and wealth here that I can in your time. No matter how much wisdom I bring them, how many slaves, how many women."

"Women?" Xander said, kicking and jerking around with renewed vigor. "Our *mother?* You brought her *here?* For what? To sell her off, to use her to bargain with?"

His foot made contact with Phemus's stomach, and the big man flinched. Phemus gave Xander's arm a quick snap that made him yelp in pain. Taksidian retrieved something from his pocket and slipped it into Phemus's mouth, as though rewarding an obedient dog with a treat. Phemus chewed happily.

"Her . . . *removal* from your house served multiple purposes," Taksidian said with a shrug. "But I have to say, I do find useful the benefits awarded to me for such offerings. A private residence, which you saw; my own slave"—he patted Phemus on the back, as a father would—"and the use of others as I need them; an occasional invitation to a party at the palace. Very entertaining."

"Where is she?" David said. "Let us see her!"

"Ah, I'm afraid some things are beyond even me," Taksidian said, waving a hand dismissively. "Prizes like her go right to the palace. Something about the American language, as spoken by females, fascinates the Atlantian royalty. Go figure."

David looked in the direction of the mountaintop castle, but hills on this side of the river blocked it. He said, "The castle, she's at the castle?"

Taksidian scowled. He used his nails to flip the hair off his face and said, "Feisty woman, your mother. I heard she disappeared, got away."

"Got away?" David said. "To where?"

"That's the problem with bringing women from other times," Taksidian said. "If they wander too close to a portal—" He whistled sharply and snapped his fingers open like a magician making a scarf disappear.

"But," David said, "how do you know she's not still here?"

"No place to hide in Atlantis," he said. "And no one goes against the royals. Anyone who saw her would catch her and bring her back." He shrugged. "Besides, outside of the castle, the portals tends to *take* people who don't belong in this time, whether they want to go or not. If I knew which world got her, I wouldn't be looking for a replacement."

David thought of the other night, when Toria heard Mom calling to her from the third-floor hallway. Someone had been using Wuzzy to lure her up there. "Leave my sister alone!" he screamed. "You . . . you . . . !"

Taksidian waved a hand at him. "Hush," he said. "Save your strength. You have a long journey ahead."

# CHAPTER

Sixty

"Atlantis?" Ed King said. "But I thought it was an enlightened society."

He and Mike Peterson had been discussing the lost civilization for the past ten minutes. They had agreed to not debate the historical accuracy of its existence and pressed on into the realm of "Let's pretend it was a real place . . . now what?"

"It probably *was* ahead of its time," Mike said. "Paleohistorians hypothesize that because of its location between the Ameircan and European continents, it was able to take technological advancements from both and synergistically expound on them, moving ahead faster than either region. Supposedly, it was centuries ahead of the rest of the world in agriculture, architecture, medicine, ship building." He shook his head. "But *enlightened*? I don't think so."

"But wasn't it Plato's perfect society?" Ed remembered that Plato had been the first to write about the mythological land, couching it in terms that had historians debating whether Plato was writing fact or fiction.

Mike laughed. "It's like that telephone game, remember?" he said. "You whisper a sentence into a person's ear, and he turns to the person on the other side of him and whispers what he heard and remembered. By the time it gets around a whole circle of people, the sentence is something completely different."

"We played that in school," Toria said. "It's funny."

Mike nodded. "The stories of Atlantis are like that, only with millions of people saying what they *think* they heard and remembered, and through hundreds of generations. Plato said *Athens* was the perfect society. He held up Atlantis as the antithesis of that." He smiled at Toria's puzzled expression. "The *opposite* of perfect. It was ruled by a group of kings who were incredibly greedy. They made their own playground out of Mount Cleito, named after the mother of Atlas, whose father was Poseidon. They forced the rest of the citizenry into poverty and servitude, destined to work solely for the benefit of the royal families. Fact is, Atlantis was a society bent on war, on conquering the European and American continents. Everything they did was about acquiring more land, more treasures, more slaves."

Ed sat back in his chair. He ran his palms over his face, trying to reign in his runaway thoughts. Is this what they faced in Phemus? A soldier from one of history's most bloodthirsty, battle-hungry societies?

He hoped the brute didn't return while the kids were in the house alone.

"But Mr. Peterson," Toria said. "What did Phemus say to me?"

"Phemus?"

"A name we made up," Dad explained, surprised that he had not asked the question himself. "The voice on the teddy bear. What did he say?"

Mike leaned back in his chair, smiling thinly. "He said, 'Have you come to play?'"

"*Play?*" Toria said.

Dad put his hand over hers. "That doesn't make sense, Mike. We thought . . . I mean, we're pretty sure it was meant as a warning or threat."

"Oh," Mike said. "No doubt it was. Considering the violent games the Atlantians engaged in to prepare their young people for war, Atlantis is the last place you want to go to 'play.'"

# sixty-one

Taksidian turned to the soldiers, who had stopped just out of range of the boys' kicking feet. *"Ayta ta agoria anikoyn sto skafos stin Athina."*

He pointed toward the road David and Xander had been heading for. Streaming from it into the square was a line of children, shackled and chained together. Their eyes were downcast, their hair messy birds' nests, their clothes nothing but rags. They shuffled forward, chains rattling, as a soldier in the front tugged on a leash and another cracked a whip behind them.

A boy in the corral of fighting children appeared at the fence. Others joined him. They were panting hard, bloody and battered. Still, they grinned and pointed at the chained kids. They began calling out, words David didn't understand. But he could tell by their tone and sharpness that they were taunts: insults hurled like rocks at kids who were already miserable.

"Your timing is impeccable," Taksidian told David and Xander. "The Atlantian fleet is just about to set sail for an assault on Athens. Never one to waste a resource, this society uses *all* its members in battle. They have found that children, mostly those captured in previous conquests or their own who show no other aptitude, come in especially handy."

He stepped close to David, grabbing his knees to stop his legs.

"Imagine," Taksidian said. "Swabbing decks, washing dishes, stocking pantries." His nails dug into David's legs, making him cry out.

"Stop it!" Xander said.

"Now, now," Taksidian said. "I'm just getting to the fun part. You'll get to witness the battle firsthand. The Atlantians always send in an advance platoon of children. It seems to confound their enemies, facing a horde of terrified kids. Once the opposing force gets over the initial shock, they expend valuable arrows and energy, while giving away their hiding spots, to clear the field."

The chain gang of children stopped beside them. Phemus lowered Xander into the arms of a soldier. They gripped him so tightly, all David could see of his brother's struggle were flexing muscles. They bound him with shackles and slipped the end of the chain through protruding hoops.

Phemus swung David around and dropped him behind his brother. A guard, still tending to Xander's shackles, reached a hand back and clamped it over David's shoulder. Phemus stepped away, giving David a clear view of Taksidian. David tried to drill holes into him with his gaze.

Taksidian merely smiled. He lifted his hand and waggled his fingers at him. "Bon voyage," he said. "I'll give my regards to your family."

David's molars ground together. He didn't know which was worse: being shipped off to a battle where he and Xander would almost certainly die, or Taksidian winning. Their disappearance would break Dad. He would either give up and leave the house to Taksidian, or he would be so defeated, so down, it wouldn't take much for Taksidian to crush him. *Crush.* David tried not to think of what that word meant, but he could not stop an image from filling his mind: men carrying stretchers out of his home's front door, white sheets covering bodies from head to toe, one Dad-sized, one Toria-sized.

David felt a fire ignite within him. It felt as though flames would burst out from every pore of his body.

The soldier holding David stooped to pick up a set of shackles. His hand slipped off David's shoulder. David lunged forward, shoving his hands into the man, toppling him.

And he ran.

CHAPTER

# Sixty-two

David dodged away from the soldier's reaching hand, kicking feet. The soldier on the far side of Xander yelled. Chains rattled, and David realized without really thinking about it that the man had jumped for him, only to be stopped by the chains between his brother and the boy in front of him.

David ran deeper into the square, heading for a gap between two vendors' stalls on the far side.

Behind him, Xander hollered, "Go, David! Run! Run!"

The words echoed in David's ears, putting energy into his legs, driving him forward. He wanted to yell back, *I'll come back for you! I'll find you!* But all he could do was run . . . and plan his maneuvers around the men in the square. They were turning toward him, scowling, pointing, moving to stop him. The two bare-chested fighters wiped blood and sweat out of their eyes and darted into David's path. He ducked below lunging arms. Another man kicked him in the ribs, a blow that sent David rolling over the cobblestones.

He scrambled up, catching sight of the kids from the fighting corral slipping between and over the fence rails and running toward him. Footsteps behind him. A glance over his shoulder showed him the three soldiers pushing past the men who had tried to catch him.

"David, run!" came Xander's voice.

He lowered his head and concentrated on pumping his legs, swinging his arms. Speed was one of his advantages on the soccer field, and he called on that talent now.

*Move! Move! Move!* he told himself.

Behind him, pounding feet, huffing breaths. The jingling of metal, probably swords in their scabbards, the thin chains that held leather armor in place.

Two men in front of the stalls on either side of the gap he was targeting turned toward him. Each held a bundle in his arms and appeared confused about what to do.

Before either could decide, David shot between them and

into the narrow space. The wooden sides of the stalls flashed past on either side. He entered a packed-earth alleyway. Stone buildings rose above him, left and right. A man sat against one of the walls, sleeping. David jumped over his legs and kept running.

The pounding feet of the soldiers grew louder and deeper, reverberating against the walls. But he thought he had put some distance between them. He could no longer hear their ragged breathing.

He passed an intersecting alley on his right, realized he should have turned into it. He approached another alley, also on the right. Without slowing he arced into it. It ended in the distance at what appeared to be a sunlit street—probably the one the chain gang of children had used to enter the square.

He had to do something before the soldiers spotted him. Doors lined the walls on both sides: homes or the back entrances of shops, he thought. He zipped past one that was open. Braking hard, he spun around and slipped into the building. The guards had not yet appeared, but their footsteps announced their nearness. He yanked on a heavy door, swinging it fast, closing it quietly. A length of wood rested in a bracket attached to the wall beside the door, aligned with a matching bracket mounted to the door. He pulled the wood until it crossed from wall to door: a lock of sorts.

On the other side of the door, footsteps beat against the

alley's dirt path. They slowed and stopped. Voices—hurried, questioning. The soldiers moved back and forth.

David pressed his palms against the door. He looked over his shoulder. He was in a cavernous barnlike room. Wood planks rose like mini-buildings everywhere. On the other side of the room an old man stood, holding a board in one hand, a hammer in the other.

David pleaded with his eyes. He said, "Shhhhh."

The man slowly lowered the board to the floor. He set the hammer on top of it. Then he turned, pulled open a door, and disappeared through it. Sunlight—not as bright as it was in the open square—came through the doorway. Beyond was a stone wall, and David realized the man had stepped into the first alley he had passed.

The door under his palms rattled. He almost cried out. Someone pounded on the door, shouted. David kept his hands pressed against the wood and watched them quiver in fear. A bead of sweat trickled from his forehead into his eyebrow, then slipped into his eye. He squeezed his lids closed.

He heard quieter pounding on other doors in the alley. The soldiers were checking every one.

The door rattled again.

*Go away*, he thought.

He noticed his breathing, fast, loud. He tried to stop his lungs from working and found he couldn't.

*Did the soldier hear it? Is that why he wasn't moving on?*

He expected the door to burst in on him. He looked down at the dirt floor, where light seeped below the door. Shadows cut through the glow in two places: legs. A fat drop of sweat fell from his face, plopped into the dirt between the shadows, and vanished. The shadows stirred and moved away, taking footsteps and the clattering of metal with them.

His legs felt rubbery. His entire body shivered.

*Get a grip, Dae.*

Movement on the other side of the door. Shadows flashing past. The soldiers weren't going away. They knew David must have entered one of the shops.

*The other alleyway,* he thought. *Slip out the way the old man had gone. Get away.*

Slowly he lifted his hands from the door, careful to not rattle it, afraid that simply moving his hands would cause the soldiers to storm through it. He lowered his arms and turned.

Three shirtless boys stood inside the doorway across the room. One had a gash on his face, bloodying his cheek. Another's ribs were black and blue. One eye of the third was swollen shut, the skin mottled in blacks and reds. Boys from the corral, the ones who had appeared so intent on killing one another. Now it seemed they'd found someone else they'd rather murder.

Wide, broken-toothed grins contrasted with their rough, battered faces. Another boy ran up behind them. Then another.

A boy slapped his palm with something in his other hand. David saw that the kid held a club, like a small baseball bat. Another boy stooped and picked up the hammer the old man had left behind. When all five had filed in, a sixth appeared behind them in the alley.

David held his hands up, palms out to them. "W-wait," he said, barely a whisper. Louder: "Wait . . . please."

The boy with the club—a stocky blond kid, shorter than the others—squinted at him. He turned to the others. *"Enas ilithios allodapos."*

They all laughed. There was no humor in the sound.

When the kid with the club turned back to David, his face was twisted in a mask of hate and fury. As if sharing a single thought, the others lost their smiles, their mouths shaping into expressions he had seen only on snarling dogs. Their muscles tensed, their knees bent. Ready to attack.

David spun around, grabbed the length of wood that bolted the door, and yanked it out of its brackets.

Behind him came the stomping of a dozen feet and a chorus of screaming rage. Shadows fell over him like night.

*Not* the end . . .

# WITH SPECIAL THANKS TO . . .

TANNER BARRETT, this book's winner of my *Dream the Scene* contest. His entry put David and Xander in the Alps, facing Hannibal's army. Good job, Tanner . . . but David and Xander aren't very happy with you!

My early readers, who help make sure this wild adventure doesn't become *too* wild or unbelievable: NICHOLAS and LUKE FALLENTINE, SLADE PEARCE, BEN and MATTHEW FORD, MADDIE WILLIAMS, ALEC OBERNDORFER, JOSHUA RUARK, and ALIX CHANDLER.

My son ANTHONY, who is an early reader, constant encourager, and just plain cool.

The rest of my family—my wife, JODI; my daughters, MELANIE and ISABELLA; and my son, MATT—for putting up with my bouts of childlike enthusiasm and artistic moodiness.

My editors: AMANDA BOSTIC, JOCELYN BAILEY, LB NORTON, and JUDY GITENSTEIN—wonderful ladies and *perfect* editors.

My publisher, ALLEN ARNOLD, and the rest of Team Nelson, especially JENNIFER DESHLER, KATIE BOND, BECKY MONDS, and KRISTEN VASGAARD—for letting me write these stories and putting them into the hands of the best readers an author could hope for.

BENTLEY BROWN and the incredible faculty and students at Parkview Baptist School in Baton Rouge—your passion for these stories is the reason I write them. And an equally loud shout-out to the teachers and kids at Einstein Elementary School in Redmond,

Wash., and two special schools in Monument, Colo.: Creekside Middle School and Lewis Palmer Middle School. (I wish I had the room to name all the educators and students who made me feel so welcome in their schools during the past year. You know who you are—thank you!)

BURKE ALLEN, JAKE CHISM, BONNIE CALHOUN, REL MOLLET, TODD MICHAEL GREENE, JEANETTE CLINKUNBROOMER, SCOTT QUINE, NANCI KALANTA, and PAUL and JENNIFER TURNER—for helping me get the facts straight, spreading the word about the Kings and their adventures, and being good friends.

1. When David is in the dark chamber of bones (with no apparent way out), he panics and imagines the worst of outcomes. Have you ever been in a situation that seemed hopeless? Were you optimistic or pessimistic about what would happen? What *did* happen? What did you learn from the experience?

2. After Dad and Xander discover his grisly "artwork," Taksidian wants to "have pie" with them. Dad thinks he's trying to find out if the Kings intend to go to the police and wants to convince them not to. Even though Taksidian might be arrested if they did turn him in, Dad decides to wait until they've found Mom. Do you agree with his decision? Talk about a tough decision you've had to make and whether you believe you made the right choice, looking back on it now.

3. The Kings find out the wall lights in the third-floor hallway help keep people from the past from entering the house by scaring them. Xander tells David it's like a skull-and-crossbones warning or a Viking symbol during their reign of terror. Can you think of other signs and symbols that scared people in ancient civilizations? What symbols frighten people *today*?

4. David finds a portal from the Dreamhouse to Taksidian's home. Dad has always said, "There are no coincidences," so . . . how do you think Taksidian got that direct portal between the two houses? Who walled it up, and why? What's the deal with all those bones?

5. Jesse talks about doing something simply because you were asked to, without necessarily knowing what the outcome of your doing it will be. Have you ever been asked to do something without

having the reason explained? Can you think of situations in which someone would be expected to act without questioning? What kind of relationship would the doer have to have with the asker to make the situation okay?

6. David is beginning to realize that the house, with its portals to the past, allows him to change history in ways that can save lives—and he *wants* to do what he can. Have you ever been in a position to make things better, even if it meant doing something scary or dangerous? What did you do? How did it turn out?

7. Keal has known the Kings for only a few days. Still, he wants to protect them and feels "something for them that might have been love." What about the Kings do you think makes him feel this way?

8. Xander and David like to talk before going to sleep. It's their way of processing the day's events, of trying to put things in perspective and calm down. Do you have a special person in your life in whom you confide and bounce ideas off of? Is there a time of day you like to "unload" your concerns?

9. Jesse studied history to help him understand the places the house took him, and Xander's knowledge of the Civil War helps the boys know that they changed history for the better. Do you like learning about historical events? What things in the past especially interest you? Why?

10. The brothers follow Phemus to an ancient civilization, a place that historians debate over whether it ever existed. What do you think: Was it a real place? What do you think the people there were like? (Plato describes it in his dialogues *Timaeus* and *Critias*.)